THE UNIVERSE IS MY SUGAR DADDY

by

Heather Hummel

PathBinder Publishing

PathBinder Publishing, LLC
Cover Design: PathBinder Publishing
www.PathBinder.com

Dear Ali,

I am so grateful our souls decided to have us meet in this lifetime, too! So excited to have you come down to Carmel

Hugs, Heather

THE UNIVERSE IS

MY SUGAR

DADDY

Preface

*T*he Universe provides us with two wells to dip into: fear and love. What one do you draw from to create your life? Your answer to this question is critical because thought is the first part of creation. As we think, we create; and therefore, our lives are the reflection of our thinking on all conscious levels."

– Anonymous

*J*ournaling is a forum for our thoughts, which in turn create our realities. So when we journal we ought to regard it as a venue for creating the lives we want. Journaling provides us with the option of choosing what to write based on two possible forms of thought: positive and negative. The words we pen are reflections of our thoughts, our desires, and our soul. Because of this we transfer our thoughts from our minds to paper, which in turn creates our realities. The result is that the thought is now etched in our minds and transferred to our subconscious. Therefore, if our journaled thoughts have the tendency toward negativity, then it will follow that our lives will perpetuate in being negative. Alternatively, if the words penned are positive, then it will follow that we will manifest our innermost desires.

As an example: "The *subconscious* is simply power without direction." (Florence Scovel Shinn, *The Game of Life and How to Play It*) Our *conscious* thoughts plant the seeds in our *subconscious*, which then create the garden of our life in tangent with the destiny of our *superconscious*. In the hierarchy of the three layers of consciousness: *conscious* thoughts are those produced in our living minds and are often formed based on exterior experiences and influences; *subconscious* thoughts are those formed by the influences of our conscious thoughts — simply put if we think negatively our *subconscious* generates negative circumstances in our lives, but if we think positively, our *subconscious* generates positive circumstances in our lives; the superconscious is our higher self, which sees and knows all. When we are in alignment with our *superconscious*, our path is readily available to us. It's as though the *conscious* is the car, the *subconscious* is the engine, and the superconscious is the destination. The car (conscious) fuels the engine (subconscious) with the goal of reaching a destination (superconscious). If the car fills the engine with negativity, it will clog the engine and wreak havoc on the possibility of reaching the intended destination. If, however, the car fuels the engine with positive thoughts, the engine will run and function at an optimal level and will hence reach its intended destination without fail.

When considering the art of journaling, consider what is put to paper as having the potential of being created...and when it is, you'll have the journal to reflect upon.

Chapter I

*Y*ear after year introduced the same process — grow, fall, rot. The crimson and golden-amber leaves lay on the ground beneath Samantha's bedroom window in a heap. Gentle fall winds stirred them, delaying them from rotting — dissolving too quickly into the ground only to eventually be replaced by next year's batch. Quite possibly the first snow fall would arrive early and take care of them, burying them in caps of white powder or heavy flakes laden with moisture. Upstairs in the loft, which consisted entirely of the master suite of her cabin, Samantha rolled over, reluctant once again to face the day. Her eyes still swollen from the flow of heavy tears shed the night before made them difficult to open. And now that the nights of crying herself to sleep and the mornings of puffy eyes had blurred into a few weeks, (or was it a month already?), she grew used to awakening slowly. She lost track of the days of the week ever since the day after her life changed. The day Robert left her and the next day when she quit her office management job marked the beginning of time when she didn't keep track of time anymore.

Having freedom from keeping to a watch and attending management meetings would normally be considered a beautiful thing, but for Samantha it represented a vast canyon of darkness and uncertainty about her future. Due to her abruptly exorbitant amount of free time, the alarm clock on her nightstand was now coated with a thin layer of dust. Hair and dust bunnies danced across the carpets, and downstairs the dishes made a nightly attempt to crawl out of the sink. Laundry was the worst of the chores—lifting the basket of clothes consumed every ounce of energy her body could muster. It wasn't supposed to be so physically draining. The end of a relationship normally didn't suck the life out of her like it did this time. She'd quit jobs before and never experienced the lethargy that consumed her body, mind and soul. The emotional tax she knew would be there, but she hadn't expected the physical weight she felt in every move of her body. Even brushing her teeth, when she finally pulled herself from bed and made it to the bathroom, meant lifting an arm above shoulder height. Dread.

Collapsing into a pile of sorrow under her covers at night took the least amount of effort. It meant she made it through another day. Another evening. Now all she had to do was find a way to sleep, but closing her eyelids— that she could do. Her recurring nightmares, when sleep dominated, immersed her body into deep wild rivers. In each dream, she'd clamor, drowning alongside the edge unable to

2

reach the crest of the river's bank. Reaching out, she'd barely feel her way through the murky, tumultuous water for the edge in the hopes of grabbing hold of a random jutted branch that might ground her, hold her weight, even if she remained under water. It would be a place to start.

Each time she awoke, normally in a sweat, from this particular dream that repeated itself during many endless nights, she feared drifting back to sleep in the off chance that the dream picked up where she left off — drowning. A dream's continuance seemed to never happen when they were good dreams. Those dreams escaped consciousness when she awoke, leaving her with only a memory of something good, something hopeful. However, it had been a long time since she experienced a dream that she wanted to resume after awaking. And last night's nightmare was no different.

*****

Samantha shocked her therapist, Ragnar Axel, when she announced to him later in that memorable week that she quit her job without giving the standard two weeks notice.

"They can fire you on the spot, so why can't I quit on the spot?" she defended. She hadn't seen him since the duo of life-changing events. "And, Robert broke up with me on the spot. Why should I owe anyone any courtesies?"

Ragnar sat in his chair and stared at her with disbelief stroked across his face. No matter how hard he tried to hide it and remain professional, Samantha read the writing in his pores. She had never before experienced him at a loss for words. This was a side of him that she would have found almost entertaining if she hadn't been clutching a Kleenex box with one hand and a wad of damp tissues in the other.

The name alone, Ragnar Axel, was what first drew Samantha to him. Asking friends or neighbors for a therapist referral is like asking to borrow their underwear, she believed. So, she only had her gut instinct to go by, and her gut loved his name. The way it sounded when she said it, so official and stoic. "Ragnar Axel," she said out loud, looking at his ad in the yellow pages months earlier. There was no photo of him in the ad, and when she met him she wondered why he didn't use one. He was handsome in his own right, even at his nearing retirement age. Some people, she knew, grew better looking with age and although she hadn't known him until now, she imagined he was one of them.

"Kind of like Sean Connery," Samantha told her best friend, Amanda, after the first session with Ragnar. "Not his looks, but the better with age concept," she further explained.

4

Although, he did have salt and pepper hair that he kept short and intriguing blue eyes that questioned you before he spoke. So, yes, the name was a start.

Little did Samantha know that when she started therapy she would meet Robert shortly afterwards. While starting therapy may have been the catalyst to meeting him, it wasn't the only reason. Her reason for calling Ragnar was to explore her history of failed relationships. By the time she dialed his number, she had tired of never making it to love, let alone the altar. In her mind she envisioned two paths — one to her version of what happiness represented, which was the one everyone else seemed to have, and the version that was her own personal reality. At least her friends and family made their peace with her situation a while ago, realizing that trying to talk "sense" into her proved fruitless.

Some of Samantha's relationships began with a bang only to end abruptly for no apparent reason, or they'd fizzle in and out due to lack of effort and interest from one or both parties. Once or twice the man *de jour* moved on before Samantha was aware the relationship had ended. Her plan when she called Ragnar was to delve into therapy before the next relationship came along so that she could resolve her issues and be better prepared for when it happened. When she first met with Ragnar, he insisted she call him Ragnar, he asked if she felt as though she jumped into relationships too fast, possibly intimidating her mates.

"In all honesty, no, I don't believe I do."

"Are you the jealous type?" he asked, continuing to probe her like a tooth until hitting a sore spot, causing a grimace.

Samantha wrinkled her face. Off hand she couldn't think of a scenario where any one of her boyfriends had given her reason to be jealous, only hurt and abandoned when they left, or nothing at all in some cases. Well, maybe a pang of guilt once or twice when she was the one who ended it.

"Maybe," an incident finally came to mind, "with Adam; His previous girlfriend called him a lot when we first started dating. It didn't bother me at the time. He treated me like a princess and convinced me quite easily that he was no longer interested in Tracy. But, I found out later that my entire relationship with him was just his trying to make her jealous, which of course worked and he went back to her."

"Did that bother you? Finding out he used you?" The dental pick dug deeper.

"Not really, but then again I haven't been tested much with that. Either I didn't care enough about the guy, or there was simply no reason to be jealous. Maybe that's part of my problem? What if I never cared enough to be jealous? That is until Robert, but that didn't end in jealousy." She shocked herself with her own epiphany.

Ragnar noted that her time was up, and Samantha left his office with enough to think about.

Curled up in bed that evening, she wrote in her journal.

> *October 25th – Met with Ragnar today. We continue to delve into my past relationships – the drudges of breakups, the emotions around jealousy, longing, and abandonment when they leave me…or my lack of emotion when I break up with them. They all bundle together in one big mess called "Samantha's relationships."*

Within the walls of his office, Samantha and Ragnar continued to discuss other possible reasons for the demise of her relationships.

"Can you pigeon-hole the type of men you've dated?" Ragnar asked one week. He tapped his foot against the coffee table between them, a habit of his that Samantha was growing used to and didn't take personally.

"Don't think so." she answered. "They've been all across the board. I've dated poets to brokers. Some rich. Some poor. Most of them were nice, at least in the beginning. I don't think I can pigeon-hole them into categories like, 'I only date jocks' or 'I only date white collars.'"

In the next session Ragnar went back to focusing on the reasons for the endings, and it was the very next day when Samantha met Robert. She and Amanda were leaving Ben & Jerry's and Robert was entering through the same door. Amanda held the door, waiting for Samantha who was grabbing a napkin from the holder.

"Hold on to your britches," Samantha said. "You know I can't eat this before it starts to drip all over the place."

"Let me help you with that," Robert said. He adeptly held the door open, relieving Amanda, and held on to the napkin container so it wouldn't slide across the counter as Samantha yanked a clump of them with her one free hand.

"Thanks," Samantha said. Robert let the door close, leaving Amanda outside with her cone watching the events unfold inside. Robert and Samantha struck up a conversation and before she left they exchanged phone numbers.

"Are you nuts?" Amanda asked when Samantha emerged from the store. Amanda held her ice cream cone in one hand and waved a motherly finger at Samantha with the other.

"What?"

"Getting the phone number of a guy you don't know."

"Why not? He's cute, polite, and likes ice cream. What's not to like so far?"

Samantha found out later what was not to like. To start with, his oversized purebred German Shepherd slept in the bed with him. There were nights when she woke up to two brown eyes looking down at her, which normally would have been romantic, but in this case the snout between the eyes was furry and the breath unbearable. Prince, as the dog was named, enjoyed nesting in the blankets. He dug them into a not-so-neat pile, circling until he was ready to make his landing, at which time he plopped his ninety-pound furry existence against her hip, and her back for that matter. Robert would go to bed joking, "Prince, you're my man. Make room for me though!" and then proceeded to squeeze his own one-hundred-ninety pound body between Prince and Samantha. Not even his king sized bed was sufficient for the three of them. But, Robert kept saying, "Isn't this great?" while cuddling in close to her.

She often wondered if he would cuddle with her as much if he weren't forced to have his body pressed up against hers. But, she had already fallen for him and since she waited a while to sleep with him, establishing that she had feelings for him, she didn't know that Prince would be a bed companion.

Samantha wondered how many girlfriends he'd lost because of the hairy bedmate. Due to her fear of failing in yet another relationship, and the way she felt about Robert outside of the bedroom, she tolerated Prince and almost grew accustomed to it to the point that she would sleep through the night—a great accomplishment.

Ragnar refrained from chuckling when Samantha sat in his office one afternoon relaying her stories about Prince. She was in tears of depression, but managed to use animated gestures in her description that nearly led Ragnar to tears as he fought back the urge to laugh. Samantha knew all along that he was fighting it, and actually played up the scenes to see if he would break. Keeping his professionalism in tact, he didn't. Instead he asked, "So, why do you think you allowed this behavior to continue for so many months?" and they would go round and round about her off the charts low-self-esteem issues. At one point, when Robert first broke up with her, Ragnar contemplated prescribing anti-depressants, but Samantha wouldn't hear of it. She was bound and determined to work through her issues while keeping her faculties intact and Ragnar respected that. She believed she was one of his more entertaining clients and didn't want to show up drugged up and unable to remember their sessions, which is how she perceived being medicated would be like.

*****

Now, waking up for the umpteenth day in a row after crying herself to sleep, the idea of medication tempted her. She curled up in as tight a ball as she could make herself into, disappointed that she couldn't disappear completely. Lifting one eyelid she looked ahead to the wall on the other side of the room. It held a stream of light across it. *Morning*, she thought. *Do I want to face this day?*

Now that she was unemployed, although becoming a writer shouldn't mean that, she could spend the entire day in bed and nobody would be the wiser. Wallowing in her misery was as tempting as the medication. Then she thought about her novel and where she left off with it. *Winter's Truth* was fast becoming her best friend and her sole purpose for stepping her feet on the area rug next to her bed each morning. It was the one thing in her life that could lure her out of bed now that she didn't have a man to lure her into bed. The issue of being in a bed at all was a constant dichotomy.

Surrendering to the day's beckoning, she squeezed herself out from under the covers. Her sheets were still the thin, cotton ones of summer. She meant to replace them with flannel ones, but hadn't mustered the energy and with the recent Indian summer, she had an excuse not to. After padding to the bathroom, she weighed herself on the digital scale in the corner, a habit she formed back in college in fear of gaining the noted freshman fifteen.

Weight fell off her in the past weeks, but she figured much of it was water weight from the tears. She never gained or lost beyond a narrow margin of seven pounds since high school. Now in her late thirties, she was thankful for at least being able to maintain her physique over the years. Her hair was another issue. It had thinned since the days of being a teen with long, thick ponytails. But considering it was quite thick before, the thinning now actually allowed her more flexibility with styles and layering that she couldn't manage before. It was the infiltration of grays into the once beautiful auburn tone that she battled, and often lost except for the few weeks after a coloring, which never matched her original color that she adored.

Someone once told her, "It's not wrinkles, but gray hair and yellow teeth. Those are the two things that'll age you." It wasn't long after that when Samantha splurged for the whitening formulas at the drug store and spent an hour a day unable to talk because her mouth was full of gooey strips filmed over her teeth. She noticed a difference in a matter of days, but with all the coffee and lattes she drank, it defeated the purpose and she couldn't be bothered to brush her teeth after each cup. She did, however, continue to indulge in the whitening process when she had extra cash and the patience to endure the goo. Since she never spent money on pedicures or manicures, teeth whitening was one luxury that she allowed herself. That and therapy were her two biggest nonessential expenses during this time in her life.

On this morning she would face neither, nor would she worry about her finances. Her sanity depended on finishing and selling her novel. The race against that clock was stronger than the race against her biological one. She gave up on the idea of being a mother a while ago and rarely revisited it because the indulgence in the thought was too discouraging. However, the possibility of not having someone special to share the glory of being a published author when the time came hung above her head. She dreamt of having a handsome husband swing open the front door to their home as she flies in stating in elation, "It sold! My book sold!" Naturally, he would scoop her up in his arms and tell her she was the most amazing literary genius of this century.

*****

"So, what are you going to do for work?" Ragnar asked during one of her post-breakdowns, also classified as an early midlife-crisis, sessions. He tugged on his beard and watched as she picked a blade of grass off the bottom of her shoe.

"I haven't told my family or friends this yet, so you're the first to know," she said. She reached over and grabbed the cup of water on

the end table next to the leather couch she was
sitting on—this after putting the grass blade in
the garbage can between the couch and the end
table. She sat on the couch because the
traditional process of lying down during
therapy gave her the creeps, and she imagined
not many people did that anymore. While
sipping the water, Samantha looked at Ragnar,
noting his patience in awaiting her answer.
They hadn't spoken much about her career
dreams and aspirations because of the initial
focus on her string of failed relationships.
Actually, she felt it was more of a rope than a
string. Or possibly a thread, since a thread is
more fragile than a string. But, rope defined
the difficulty through the nature of its
thickness, heaviness.

"I'm following my dream," she started
after taking one last sip and replacing the cup
on the wet ring it left on the table's corner.

"Dream?" Ragnar raised an eyebrow at
her. Obviously his interest was more piqued
than it had been prior to the water sipping
delay, and in hindsight, Samantha wished she
had waited until this moment to sip it. To
drink it now though would have been too
obvious that she was toying with him and a
waste of time and money. After all, she was
paying cash for her appointments since she
gave up her medical insurance when she quit
her job. It wasn't that she enjoyed egging him
on, but it was a bit of a game that she had

developed to keep him on his toes, quite possibly because he was one of the few men that she had undivided attention from and because she was able to control the outcome of their time to a degree. As a therapist, he was interested in her and she wasn't used to that, even if she was paying him.

"Yes, my dream. I've wanted to be one since I first learned how to do it."

"And that would be?" Tap, tap, tap of his foot.

"A writer. I've always wanted to be a writer." Samantha sat and waited for the debate to begin. The one she had with her family in high school when she announced she wanted to be a photojournalist. Their lack of support left her confused and sent her off track, never quite recovering her balance--until now.

"You'll never make it," they had said, "the shot of making it big is one in a million." And that was the response she waited for from Ragnar.

On some level she looked forward to the debate because even in her fragile mindset she was determined to turn the desolate outcome that all had predicted and to rewrite her future. Proving Ragnar and the others wrong was only part of it though; writing was her passion and it was what had kept her sane over the years, kept her off the medications.

"How can I focus on my writing if I'm on medications?" she would ask Amanda, a pediatrician, rhetorically. "Even over-the-counter cold medications leave me disoriented." Samantha's resilience to medication was too low, and her dream of being a writer was too high. She wouldn't succumb.

Instead of the refutation she expected, Ragnar said, "Good! That's a terrific goal. What makes you love writing so much?"

Stunned by his response, Samantha had to think for a minute before answering him. No one had ever asked her why she loved writing. A formulated answer didn't exist and she needed time to consider how she would explain her innate love for the written word. She only knew it in her heart and her love for writing hadn't mattered enough to anyone else before. She reminded herself that he was there for the purpose of caring, but still, his response seemed genuine and so her answer must reflect as such.

"It's just something that I feel I'm good at, that I love doing, so that's a start. But, it also takes me to places outside of my own life, you know? Except for when I journal. That's too much of a reflection of my own life at times. They can be pretty scary to go back and read." It was the best she could come up with under the circumstances of his response.

"Has it helped? The journaling?"

"Yes, it's insightful I suppose. I don't go back and read my entries unless I'm having a good day though. Sometimes I laugh at how down I was a month ago or a year ago on a particular day. But, most of the time it just saddens me."

"What else do you write?"

"I've started a novel. But other than that, just some poems and short stories since those are what I've had time for while working a desk job."

"That sounds great. What are your plans for making this a career?"

She knew that question was coming. The doubt had to ease its way into the conversation at some point. The idea of making an actual living as a writer always loomed in people's minds. Just once, she'd like for someone to not doubt her, even with the underlying questions such as this one, which she translated as, "So, just how are you going to make money doing this writing thing?" and it frustrated her.

"I'm working on it. I'm taking it one day at a time since I kinda just broke up with Robert *and* quit my job. All I know is that this is what I have to do. It's all I want to do."

What she wanted to do was scream, "I'll write my books then I'll sell my books...how else!" but she kept it to her in-the-box answer. The energy to defend was too much for her at this point, even if it was directed at her therapist.

"Okay. Well, maybe it's a good idea to take some time and focus on your book. Then you can go back to work when your head's clear and you're ready." Ragnar made yet another note on his pad of paper.

"Weren't you listening?" Samantha squealed. "This is my new work. I'll never step foot in an office as an employee again." This time Samantha surprised herself with the tone of her voice. Looking down at her feet, she was sorry she lashed out at him. "Sorry. But, you're the one person who's supposed to believe in me. If anything because I pay you to."

"You pay me, yes. But your welfare is also my best interest. We'll continue this next week. Time's up," Ragnar said.

"Next week." Samantha hoisted herself from the couch. Moments later she walked out onto the sidewalk. She felt a sense of freedom after having shared her secret with confidence, despite Ragnar reluctance to have faith in her. He would just be one more person she'd have to prove herself to. But, the voice in the back of her head reminded her that proving her goal was no one's business in the end.

Chapter II

$\mathscr{T}$he only envelope in Samantha's mailbox at the end of the week was her last paycheck. Tempted to stick it on the refrigerator for both prosperity purposes and for a rainy day, she instead, stuck it inside her wallet. Part of her didn't want to be constantly reminded of the desk job that nearly drove her to insanity, just as her boyfriends had, and a larger part of her knew that the bills would keep coming in even though the money wouldn't be.

The company she left was a small manufacturer that could have made widgets for all she cared. In charge of the day-to-day operations, Samantha opened the mail, paid the bills, deposited the receivables, ordered supplies, and took care of anything that systematically went wrong.

After four years of employment with that company, it was a euphoric experience to walk out the door without a glance over her shoulder or a pause in her step. Parking lot air never smelled so fresh. She climbed into her car, drove to the nearby lake and stared at the reflection of the remaining foliage. The still lake sparkled with a glass layer above its murky belly. That's how she felt that day...coated in glass — if she made a move she would shatter and her own murky underbelly

19

would be exposed to the world, and even more frightening at the time, exposed to her.

Truth was she was an awful office manager. Numbers, spreadsheets, credits and debits not only bored her, but they had no place in her head. Instead of focusing on those, she found herself reading and editing every word that came across her desk. She once found a typo on an invoice of a company that reportedly just spent hundreds of thousands of dollars changing their corporate image. Their new preprinted invoices displayed the company logo at the bottom, and there, for all editorial eyes to see, was a glaring typo. Samantha knew someone in the accounts receivable department and took the liberty to call attention to it. The next invoice that came in reflected the change; Samantha only smiled after paying the bill and filing it away.

There were many days when she felt like she was under the scrutiny of her manager, Rick. He started out low on the company's family tree, but managed to bond with his boss over their common interest in Dungeons and Dragons.

"Dungeons and Dragons?" The words spit off Samantha tongue. "You're kidding, right?" She pressed one hand on her desk and tilted the rockable desk chair away from Rick as though the diseased hobby was contagious.

"Hey, don't knock it. The boss is into it too," Rick said.

Samantha was appalled that grown men had an interest in what she perceived simply as little battling toys that were meant for boys, not grown men. She felt ashamed for them when they dared to discuss it in public, as they displayed no sense of shame themselves. But, Rick Christianson found the soft spot of his boss, worked it over for a few years, and held the record for never calling in sick. Rick became the boss' go-to man and his annual reviews glowed to the point that Samantha swore she saw light coming out of the personnel filing cabinet drawer labeled "C."

Rick was determined to keep his squeaky clean reputation and was known to come down on the plebeians below him, especially when the big boss was absent from the office. Often asking Samantha, "Has this bill had been paid?" "Had that invoice gone out?" "Were there more ink cartridges on order?" No matter what the question, Samantha shoveled him a deflective answer that bought her time to complete the task or fix the problem, which was why she was able to muddle through for so long. Most of the time Rick didn't know what he was asking for, he was merely posturing, and she knew it.

In past positions when she felt her job was in jeopardy, Samantha sought new employment before leaving. She discovered over the years that personality in an interview was often enough to be offered a job on the spot. They rarely checked references, which she always listed as "available upon request" and used Amanda in a pinch. Somehow fourteen years of doing this became her way of life, but it also sucked the life out of her.

Like Samantha's previous bosses, Rick was surprised when she quit. He had more employees under his thumb than he could handle, a situation he camouflaged well. It was common for at least a few employees a day to wiggle out from under his pressing thumb and make a mistake that went unnoticed until it snowballed into a mass that left a trace resembling a tangle of cables under a desk — unable to detangle. When these mistakes came to his attention, and if it either had the potential to ruin him or if it was bad enough, he took grand pleasure in showing the employee to the door, wiping his hands together in glee as they went to their car with their cardboard box of personal items under one arm.

But, when someone left for brighter horizons, Rick took it personally. Samantha quit right at noon. She spent the morning with her office door closed, a gesture that neighboring employees knew meant to leave her alone while she did the balance sheet and monthly reports. She deleted all of her personal files off the computer that she didn't need, and then copied her resume, a few short stories she had written on slow afternoons, and most importantly — her novel, to a flash drive that she kept stored in her purse.

Putting her entire future on a tiny drive that was no bigger than a pack of gum felt odd, and stashing it in her purse felt sinister. Next she emptied her desk of personal items, some of which she tossed in the garbage: Post-It notes with phone numbers of men she would never call again, a tampon that ended up so far in the back of her drawer that the paper wrapper had torn and she was sure it wasn't sanitary any more, a bottle of expired Ibuprofen that she brought over from her last job, hand lotion, a mug that was a birthday present from Amanda two years ago, and a few pens that she accumulated.

Once that was done, she sat and stared at the back of the closed door. A calendar hung on it noting different employee's vacation days and birthdays. As office manager, she was required to track this information, making sure no one's vacations overlapped, which would leave Rick's knickers twisted up to his pin sized head, and that everyone's birthday was recognized in the event they didn't have a family or a spouse to give recognition. Really these office celebrations were an excuse to escape cubicles and indulge in cake.

Staring in a trance at the weeks ahead, she ran the dialogue through her mind. "It's simple, really. I quit," was the most tempting approach. How could anyone argue with that?

The sticky part of it all was that she wasn't giving the industry standard two weeks notice. She knew they'd replace her quickly and the probability of them working her to death for the next two weeks, hovering over her every move to make sure all was in order for the next sucker, was more than she could face. The murky soil beneath the fragile glass coating of her files and paper trails couldn't handle the pressure of their intrusion anymore than she could. It would crack and shatter, like an antique porcelain doll thrown down a flight of stairs, and in turn it would crack and shatter her. The ripple effect was inevitable and her personal life was already smashed to smithereens.

There was no way she'd allow Rick to add to the damage. This left her with the dilemma of how to quit without giving notice and without exposing her underbelly. A sick relative? A sudden job offer in another state — she needed to pack? Then she realized her most valuable piece of ammunition that could not be used in the game of Dungeons and Dragons. She was a woman.

"It's a female thing, Rick. I'm really not comfortable going into details. But, you know how much I enjoyed working here, and I'm sure you'll find a terrific replacement." There she said it.

The words swirled around the now quiet room. Rick went to speak more than once, but each time couldn't find the words and at the end of the conversation, he simply said, "Okay." Samantha made a mental note to keep that line in mind; there were other opportunities when it might come in handy. Most of the employees were at lunch when she exited his office; this allowed Samantha the opportunity to quietly exit through the rear door to her car, down the street, and to the lake before anyone would know.

"Are you out of your mind?" Amanda insinuated more than asked. When Samantha returned home later that afternoon, she called the one person whom she thought might understand.

"Why? It was just a job." Samantha defended her actions over the phone. Amanda was still at her office. She had been the town's favorite pediatrician for years, but never married, let alone birthed children of her own. Her pearly white teeth, slick black hair, and flawless skin, save for the one freckle under her left eye that was more endearing than distracting, made her the ideal candidate for making others guess she had to be someone's wife and should definitely be reproducing genes.

"Have you told Ragnar yet? What about your family?"

"No and no," Samantha said. "I don't see Ragnar until Thursday, and I'm not going to tell my family until after I talk to him."

"What if they call you at work?"

"Won't happen. Mom's at a spa in Arizona, Dad never picks up the phone unless it's ringing, and even that's a stretch, and Jane is too caught up with her dissertation to care what I'm doing."

"Sounds like you have your bases covered, but what are you going to do about a job now?"

"We'll see. I'm still considering my options."

"Options? What options? You make it sound like you've got people lined up at your door waiting to hire you. Kinda like those commercials where they're all lined up to take the couple's mortgage applications."

"Funny. But that's not what I mean. I mean I might change careers."

"And do what?"

"Look, I've gotta run. I want to start cleaning out my house. You know I always need to clean when I break up with someone. It's part of my therapy."

"You quit your job because of Robert, didn't you? You freaked out and quit."

"Don't worry. I just need an overhaul. I'll be okay once I figure out which end is up."

Samantha hung up and looked around her house. She had saved enough money over the years to put a down payment on a small cottage in the country. At just over 1,100 square feet, it was what the ad referred to as "cozy." Or was it "quaint" being that it was in the country? Either way, the mortgage was affordable and it worked for the time being. Best of all, it didn't take long to clean and the bathrooms had already been updated prior to her purchasing it.

Now, having found her way out of bed, Samantha continued to the bathroom and took a look in the mirror before picking her electric toothbrush out of its holder. The puffiness around her eyes suggested that she ought to consider using cucumbers. She thought she had read or seen somewhere that they helped to reduce swelling. The toothpaste oozed out onto the brush the same way she squeezed herself out of bed. The whirl and the energy of the electric brush proved a bit unbearable so early in the morning, but since it helped to wake her up, she conceded to using it. Her old manual toothbrush sat on the edge of the sink. She wasn't sure why she hadn't thrown it out yet. It couldn't be worthy of stroking across her teeth anymore, but she kept it just in case.

The second bedroom in her cottage served as a storage room filled with the domestic items she never intended to use, yet didn't dare part with either: A sewing machine, buried under a stack of fabrics, stood against the wall under a window. The curtains were usually closed, but had they been opened, it wouldn't have mattered since the pile of fleece, cotton, and flannel blocked much of any incoming light. A quilt that an ancestor made in the late 1800s sprawled across the twin bed in the corner of the room. Bookshelves lined the wall next to the closet; while her novels, textbooks, and other readables sat on the bookshelves, the top shelf of the closet stored a chronological stack of journals from the previous seven years — chronicled by the simple matter that when she finished the pages of one, she placed it on top of the last one.

In Samantha's last meeting with Ragnar they determined that she ought to read through her old journals to see if any patterns had subconsciously developed.

"That sounds like a real pick-me-upper," Samantha said when he suggested it.

"Actually, it could be an eye opener. Try it. If there's anything in particular that you want to share, bring it in."

Ragnar's optimism that day spread across the room and slowly seeped into Samantha's veins. By the end of the session, she found herself looking forward to the trip down memory lane. After she left his office, the idea to take notes in a new journal, as though doing so would function as a "not-to-do list" for the next relationship, crossed her mind. She stopped at the stationery store down the street to pick one out. The journal she chose was smaller than her previous ones, but wore a beautiful red leather coat and in very simple lettering on the front, it stated "JOURNAL."

Samantha had been keeping the new journal in the outer pocket of her laptop bag until she was ready to delve into the old ones. Seven years, or 364 weeks, had the potential to be overwhelming to read through. She decided to start from the beginning since that would be the best way to determine a precedent or developing trend. The first journal, dating back to when she was in her mid-twenties, was a present from her aunt. The interior pages were lined, a requirement of all of her journals, as opposed to the type one might sketch artwork in. At the time of receiving the journal, she thought the exterior floral pattern to be beautiful. Even though it had been stored in a dark closet, on this day it looked as though it had been sun-faded.

Samantha was a self-proclaimed terrible artist. "I can write, but don't ask me to draw," she'd tell people. "Much beyond a stick-figure is about all I can do," she'd say, but, that was fine with her; she loved writing, but also dabbled in photography when the visual side of her artistic talents was sparked. Some of the journals displayed pictures of ex-boyfriends pasted on the tattered pages, some sported images of landscapes, creating a muse for a poem or short story. She normally wrote poems in a separate book, but if the poem matched an experience she wrote about in one of her journals, she'd write it on the same page.

Deciding on the first two journals, Samantha pulled them down carefully so as not to encourage the entire stack to fall on her head. She tucked them into her laptop bag, along with the blank new leather one and headed out to her favorite coffee shop. She determined the night before that she would read them in public with the idea that she would be less likely led to tears in the company of others.

The coffee shop was a mom and pop establishment on the corner of Main Street and Hemlock in town. Harmon was one of those towns that was small enough where everyone eventually grew to know or at least recognize one another, but not so small that they felt obligated to protect the mom and pop shops from corporate America. The lines spewing from the doors of the three Starbucks in town at 7:30 a.m. proved that.

Samantha's nature, however, was to send her business to the local entrepreneurs. She felt good when she purchased her coffee and banana bread from them rather than being just another grunt in corporate America. The local flavor who frequented the mom and pop shop, Lattes with Love, flaunted the more esoteric members of the community, which helped to inspire Samantha's writing; some of her best characters were offshoots of people she spotted in line for their latte or sitting at a table eating a sandwich, which was freshly made behind the counter, not pre-made and wrapped in plastic that corroded the flavor.

The small table in the corner was often available because it only had one seat and i seemed that not many people went to a coffee shop alone. Samantha determined that coffee drinkers normally met other coffee drinkers after a previous conversation that started with, "Hey, let's do coffee and talk about that." She wondered how many brilliant ideas were spawned over coffee. The rest of the shop-goers were a myriad of dates, girl-talks, and the occasional book club or writing group that critiqued one another's work. The writing groups were easy to determine because they each held the same manuscript in their hands, but each copy was marked in different places with different notations and with different pen colors. Samantha considered finding a group to join, but put it off because she wanted to focus solely on writing her own novel; she didn't want to read, let alone critique, other writings, especially while she was still swimming in sorrow. The potential of other writers squelching her dreams wasn't appealing.

On this particular fall day, Lattes with Love was quiet. Two elderly men sat at a table with blue prints spread out in front of them, and a woman with her young children stood in line. Samantha took her normal seat in the corner by unloading her journals, pens, and purse on it and brought only a five dollar bill with her to the front counter.

"Good morning," she said. The employee behind the counter looked as though he already had a few lattes himself. His dark, curly hair flopped across his forehead and over one eye.

"What'll you have today?" he asked.

Samantha nearly laughed every time she heard the voice of a college student. It seemed that they all took on the same voice; their slow tongues with low pitches emerged from between their lips like her toothpaste had that morning, and for that matter, the way she escaped the rapture of her covers and pillow. Had their voices been hooked up to monitors, they would be considered flat-liners and the doctors would clamor around calling, "Code Blue!" His "what'll" began with a sound that likened a barge, barely in the distance and by time he reached "today," the barge was docked and the lines were being dropped. She supposed that as a writer, analyzing words, dialog or written, came with the territory.

"A skinny latte with two pumps of peppermint, please," Samantha said with a purposeful pitch to contrast his.

"What," he started, "size?"

"Oh, a large please." 'Venti' was reserved for those other shops.

Fortunately, their service was quick despite the dialect, and it wasn't long before she was sitting at her table opening her first journal. Through the window behind her, the sun cast a shadow of her shoulder across the page, cutting the glare and making the faded ink easier to read. The ink, originally black, had faded to a tinge of gray. Samantha sat back, prepared for the memories that were to come, and took another sip of her latte before setting into the words on the pages.

> *November 1, 1998: Just got home from a date with John. This was our second. Not sure why I'm writing about this, but since this journal is new, I had to start somewhere. He took me to Paul's Pizza Place for dinner then we went to see 'The Waterboy,' which was hysterical. John held my hand, but whenever he laughed, which was a lot, he let go to slap his knee. It got to be annoying by the middle of the movie, so at one point I resumed eating my popcorn to keep my hand busy enough that he couldn't grab hold of it again. After the movie, we ran into some friends of his from college. They seemed nice, but he didn't introduce me to them.*

33

Finally one of them asked him who I was, and he just said my name, but didn't give me theirs. Not a good impression on a second date. Maybe the third will be better.

Samantha remembered John to be tall and beefy. She thought he played some college football, but not notably so. As she would read in another entry a few pages later, they did make it to a third date before he told her he didn't want to see her "like that" anymore. She lifted her latte to her lips and re-read that entry one more time, proud of herself for remaining neutral as Ragnar encouraged her to do.

There were several weeks between the time when John ended and when Samantha met Shawn. He was slender and was a poet. Samantha thought he had potential over the others because of his natural nurturing side. They went to a play on their first date at the local community theatre and afterwards she wrote:

December 2, 1998: Shawn and I had our first date today. We had to wait until after Thanksgiving since it was our first date and the holidays muddle these things. He took me to see 'Anything Goes' and apparently he thought the same of our date. I made the mistake of wearing a low cut shirt that

34

happened to match my skirt. It was under my sweater, but the theater was warm and after I removed the sweater, I do believe he spent more time with his eyes on my cleavage than he did watching the play. Hope his cheap thrills were worth the $20 he spent on the tickets. So much for my romantic poet. I told him after the play that I was having a reaction to the musty playhouse and had to go home. Hoping he doesn't call again. Back to square one of the game of my perpetual man-hunting life. There must be human life out there in the form of a male? I just don't meet them.

The holidays came and went without another date. 1999 was the first New Year that she hadn't woken up with a man sprawled out next to her since college. She marveled on the pages of the journal at how that could have been. How could she be alone and pushing thirty? It wasn't supposed to be that way she had noted.

After reading that line, she pulled out her new red leather journal and wrote, "Note to self: Line up a New Years date before Christmas!"

That didn't leave her too many more weeks and with Robert still flowing through her system she didn't know how she'd accomplish that. She put her pen down on the table alongside the journals, turned and stared out the window. The sun had made its way to the other side of the building and wasn't resting its rays on her shoulder anymore. The sidewalk was filled with people starting to break from their nine-to-fivers for lunch; she figured these were the ones who had to meet someone exactly at noon since it was just shy of striking twelve. The church down the street rang its bell twelve times on the twelfth hour and once on each half hour. The eleven thirty single ring had rattled her out of her deep concentration.

Now, at noon, the twelve rings gave her pause for reflection of her readings. How was it that she had always been so miserable? She was attractive with her auburn hair, cocoa brown eyes, and she was funny. She hadn't experienced problems *meeting* men. Intelligence and athleticism were not an issue, although it could be that her combination of both sent some men back to their video games. She wouldn't want the type who didn't appreciate those qualities of hers anyway.

Samantha reached over and picked up her purse from the chair. Before entering the shop, she had set her cell phone on vibrate so as not to be rude. There was one man she dated, Bobby, who never shut off his phone, or at least the ringer, while in a restaurant. It rang for all to hear and all eyes rested on them when the 'William Tell Overture' chimed throughout. The man at the table next to them had just bent down on his knees to propose to his girlfriend when Bobby's cell went off. Not only did it ring on the loudest setting, but he answered it and absorbed himself in a conversation with his caller. Samantha sat there and crumpled her napkin in her hands beneath the table, but she really wanted to crumple his phone and toss it into the nearby fountain. Bobby was clueless of his own rudeness and the man on his knee endured, not wanting to make more of scene by addressing Bobby's offensive behavior or to upset his girlfriend. Samantha excused herself to the ladies room and, on her way, handed the waiter her credit card and asked him to send a nice bottle of wine to the couple's table anonymously. She then left the restaurant and didn't return the one phone call she received from Bobby the next day. Manners were one thing she didn't have time to teach.

A group of men entered the coffee shop and took the table next to Samantha, snapping her back to the present moment. They were discussing their upcoming weekend plans. One drank straight-up black coffee, another drank an espresso, and the third a latte. Samantha wondered if she could classify men by the hot drink they drank. She picked up her journal and wrote down a brief description of each man along with their selected drink.

> *Man 1: Tall, salt and pepper hair, a bit stocky, but in good shape. Nice eyes. No wedding band. Black coffee.*

She always noted whether or not a man wore a wedding band. Occasionally there would be a white stripe of skin indicative of a tan line. Whether they were recently divorced or trying to camouflage the fact that they were married, neither interested Samantha.

> *Man 2: Medium height. Bald spot surrounded by black hair and a few grays. Brown puppy dog like eyes. No wedding band. Espresso.*
>
> *Man 3: Medium height. Wedding band. Blonde, tightly cut hair. Blue eyes. Latte."* It figured that the best looking one was married.

Samantha listened in on their conversation, although they wouldn't have noticed because they were too engrossed, and she nodded her head into her journal as she took notes.

"I've got a second date with Jenny this weekend. Thought I'd take her hiking and see how she does on the trails. You know, put her to the test," Man 1 said.

"Be careful. Chicks say they like hiking then you get them out there and they complain about their feet hurting or the mosquitoes or whatever they can think of," said Man 2.

"I don't know. Liz loves hiking. We take the kids all the time," Man 3 piped in between sips of latte.

"Yeah, well Liz is not your everyday woman," Man 2 said.

Man 1 listened to his two friends but glanced over at Samantha. She felt his eyes on her, looked up and smiled at him. Not sure if he knew she heard them, she shrugged her shoulders and went back to jotting down notes.

"Well, it's the second date, and I just thought it would be a nice thing to do," he concluded.

Their conversation changed over to football and a little bit about work. Samantha took copious notes, but had no idea what she would do with them. Maybe in another five years she would be sitting at the same table re-reading them as she was her old journals.

Chapter III

$\mathcal{T}$he first time Samantha walked into Ragnar's office she was more than nervous. She had never been in therapy before and considered her childhood quite normal. She and her sister shared a room without many incidents and both of her parents did the best they could raising them. Her father was an insurance broker who eventually branched out on his own and was quite successful in his field. Her mother had been a stay-at-home mom until the girls reached middle school, at which time she took a part-time job with a catering service. The hours were flexible and she was able to do much of the work in her own kitchen. Her sister, Jane, was two years older than Samantha and when they were in high school the caterer often used them as servers for events. Jane quickly grew tired of it because most of the events were filled with older people who complained a lot. She took a job in an ice cream store where she met lots of patrons and co-workers who were her own age. Samantha hadn't minded the catering though. It was better money than retail, and she learned that if she wanted a tip, she just had to smile and ignore anyone who was rude. Most events ran for about four hours, and there was a clean up crew who did, what she thought, was the worst part of the job. Once the food was eaten and the dishes cleared off the tables, she could leave.

Ragnar asked Samantha about her family during their first session and she reiterated the basics. He took dubious notes and nodded quite a bit. She had done most of the talking that day so that he could get to know her, but it felt a bit awkward and as though she didn't gain as much from it. She divulged information without any startling revelations. She left exhausted from having done all of the work and wondered if she had made the right decision to begin therapy.

"It takes time," Amanda told Samantha that night. "He has to get to know what's in your head so he can shrink it."

"Very funny. But, I guess you're right. He doesn't know me from Adam. God, remember Adam? What a jerk he was."

It wasn't until the third session that Ragnar piped in more and asked her detailed questions and followed her answers with verbal observations. She still wasn't overly confident that it was helping when she left the office. Finally, on the fourth visit, they began discussing her boyfriends and she felt they were getting to the meat of it all. Like the journals, they went through each one chronologically.

"Tell me how you met and how each one ended. You can say if they were unusually long or short relationships," Ragnar said with his pen in hand ready to jot down comments on his legal pad. She thought the fact that he had a legal pad was funny, since the previous weeks, he only used a little note pad. He pulled it from the drawer of his antique desk that sat kiddie-corner from his chair and behind the couch. The top of the desk held a pen holder, a desk blotter, and a photograph of him and his wife on a white, sandy beach somewhere and another photo of the Axel kids in their back yard. They were lying in a leaf pile looking up at the camera. *A true Kodak moment*, Samantha thought when she first saw it. Ragnar had seen her looking at it and said, "Those are my three boys. Do you want kids?"

"That's a loaded question that we better save for now," Samantha replied and sat down. Now, on their fourth session, she admitted that she wanted kids at one time but had put the thought in the back of her head.

"Why's that?" Ragnar asked.

"Because, what's the point? If I can't find a decent man to marry me why should I torture myself with wanting kids?"

"Do you see it as torture?"

"No. I see not finding the right man as torture. Not having kids is a side-effect of it all."

"I see," he said and wrote more notes. Samantha hoped that someday she could read everything that he wrote on that pad. She was certain it was more than just noting the words she had spoken. He could have written about how pathetic she was for all she knew.

About the time they had made it through her list of old boyfriends — for the fifth visit she brought a list so it would be easier to remember — was the day she met Robert.

"I don't know what it is about him that's so different from the others. I mean, I know he's more stable and grounded than the rest were, but it's more than that," she said when she met with Ragnar after her second date with Robert. They had been to dinner twice and were planning on staying in at his house for a movie the next weekend.

"What does he do?" Ragnar asked.

"He's a graphic artist for one of the local papers. I think he's one of the more senior ones, too."

"So he's creative?"

"Seems to be. He's great on the computer too. They have to know all of those fancy programs now."

"So you met at Ben & Jerry's, then who called first?"

"I called him. But, I waited a few days. I didn't want to be too anxious," Samantha fiddled with her purse strap. "He sounded happy to hear from me. We went out the next night for pizza. That was a Thursday. We went out again on Saturday for Thai. He had some family thing on Friday night."

"Does his family live here?" Ragnar tried to not sound accusational in questioning Robert's excuse, but Samantha picked up on a hint of it.

"Yes, his parents are divorced and he was helping his mom with some stuff at her house."

"Okay, so you've been out twice. What do you think you need to do from here on out to make this work as best as you can. You can't help his actions, but how can you be sure this goes the way you want it to, assuming you do want it to?"

"Oh, I want it too. It's funny; I wrote in my new journal last night that I can't believe I've met someone so great. I've never met someone like him before. Of course, I know it won't last, so I'm trying to figure out how to make it good while we are together."

"Well, think about what you want from this relationship and how what you've learned from the past can change the course of this one. Until next week keep it all in stride." Ragnar flipped the pages of notes back down onto the pad until the top sheet was exposed again. Samantha picked up her purse, pulled a check out for Ragnar and put it on his desk while he noted her time slot for the next week on his calendar.

"See you then," Samantha said and went out to her car.

Later that evening Samantha lay in bed and thought about what Ragnar said she should consider. Just what did she want from this relationship? Her nightstand table displayed a blue lamp, a red candle and her latest journal. She decided to organize her thoughts on paper instead of letting them swim in her head. This particular journal was about a third of the way full; she turned to the next available blank page. At the top she wrote, "What I want in this relationship:" followed by the series of numbers one through ten. Then she sat and stared blankly at the page for a moment before the ideas came to her.

> 1.   *I don't want it to end before we become one of those couples who have pictures of vacations and trips together. Like enough that would fill an album. I've never had that.*
>
> 2.   *I don't want him to want to spend every Thursday night with the guys. That's lame and when Adam did that to me I hated it.*
>
> 3.   *I want him to say he loves me first. The ones who have said it to me only said it after I did. (Note to self: Don't drink and say, "I love you.")*
>
> 4.   *I want him to introduce me to his family and friends as his girlfriend when I meet them.*
>
> 5.   *I want him to send me flowers at work so that all the bitches in the office know I have*

*a great boyfriend. I hate it when
they all get flowers on
Valentine's Day and are smug
about it.*

*6. I hope he likes to surprise
me with stuff. Anything as long
as it's good and a surprise.*

*7. I want him to want to meet
my family. But, that won't
happen until I'm ready.*

*8. I want him to be okay with
the idea of me being in therapy
because I don't want to hide it
from him. But, I don't want him
to think I'm nuts.*

*9. If it doesn't work out, I
want to be the one to break up.
It sucks being the breakee.*

10. I want to be in love.

After the tenth entry, Samantha sat back
and re-read her list. She was spontaneous with
her answers and wrote from past experiences.
She had a good idea of what she didn't want
and decided, that knowing this, she could
create what she did want. Before she put her
journal down and shut off the light, she took
one last look at her cell phone. No missed calls.
No voicemails. Robert hadn't known she was
meeting with Ragnar earlier, but they didn't
have plans until the next night anyway. She
decided it was good to not talk to him, that she
was given the time to reflect on her wants and

now she had a list to bring to Ragnar. He ought to be proud of her.

The journal dropped to the floor next to the nightstand and she blew out the candle, which was nearing the point of needing a new wick. She shut off the light and lay in the dark thinking about her date with Robert the next night. It would be her first time going to his house, as they had only been out in public so far. He was selecting the movie, and she was picking up dinner. Neither one wanted to cook just yet. She knew she didn't want to cook at his place without knowing what he had or didn't have for cookery, let alone to come across as being domesticated in his home, so she offered to pick up food.

"The date at his house went okay," she told Ragnar the next week. "He rented 'Funny Farm' with Chevy Chase. Great movie since it has a writer in it. I picked up some salads and prepared chicken breasts from Whole Foods and watched the movie. It was nice except his dog was always in our way."

The next few weeks of dating Robert went the same way with casual dinners and some movies at his house. It was fine, cozy and immediately comfortable like an old pair of shoes. Now, at a month into the relationship, she was settling in and taking it all in stride, even coping with Prince. They experimented with some intimacy, but that too was slow to take off. She thought him old fashion and a gentleman in that department. That made him endearing.

"What do you mean you haven't had sex?" Amanda asked one Saturday morning.

"We haven't. That's all."

"Isn't that kinda strange after a month? Have you even talked about it?"

"No. Not really. We've fooled around though." Samantha hadn't thought of it as odd until Amanda put it as so. She wasn't comfortable talking to Ragnar about that part of the relationship, not in detail anyway, and hadn't bounced it off anyone.

"Well, it's time to jump the relationship to the next level. Get the dog out of the bed first though." Amanda swung her ponytail as she entered the door to Target. They were running errands together, as they often did to keep each other company.

Samantha stopped in the doorway and contemplated Amanda's assessment. Were they taking it too slow? She hadn't thought so and now she was left with the predicament.

"Either talk about it tonight, or just go for it," Amanda said and pulled on Samantha's arm to get her through the doorway so that the elderly lady behind them could enter.

Somewhere during that evening's date with Robert, Samantha tried to bring up the subject, then she tried to make some moves on him, but both attempts were thwarted by one thing or another. Prince whined to go out

48

when she began to talk about it, and then his phone rang when she moved in closer to him on the couch. Later on they were laughing at the television show they were watching, and he put his arm around her during the commercials. She chalked those moves up to a healthy relationship and left it at that. When she left just after midnight, he kissed her goodnight at her car and closed the car door when she sat down in the driver's seat.

"We're normal, right Ragnar?" Samantha spent the days leading up to her next therapy session wondering just that. The fact that they were still together and everything was comfortable was a good sign.

"Do you think you're normal?" he deflected.

"Sure. We have fun. He's affectionate. But we haven't done much physically, if you know what I mean."

"Is that different from previous relationships?"

"Yes. For me anyway. I don't know about him."

"Have you asked him?"

"Asked him? About sex? No. I figured it would just happen. But all of our dates are the same. He doesn't seem to want much more, but he's not backing away either. We're in limbo, and I'm kind of afraid to move it one way or the other because this is nice,"

Samantha explained. "It's nice to be like an old married couple for a while."

"Married? Is that what you want from this?"

"I don't know. It's just a cliché."

"Some relationships take time to take off; others already know where it's going. It just depends on the dynamics of the couple. If you're comfortable and things are okay by your standards, then you might want to give it time."

"Yeah, give it time. It'll work out."

Samantha didn't know at the time that it wouldn't be long before it was over. How could she? Robert always led her to believe the relationship was on the right course. Until that day. That Monday morning when he sent her an e-mail. She couldn't believe he broke up with her through an e-mail. She hadn't pegged him as such a coward. And since it was early in the week, it was days before any weekend plans. It's a cardinal rule not to break up with someone until the weekend so that they didn't have to face work. She was so caught off guard that she didn't know how to respond, so she simply didn't and her next appointment with Ragnar wasn't until Thursday.

That night, between tears and phone messages to Amanda, she decided to quit her job the next day. She needed a drastic change to shake up her life. She would have moved if she had enough money and a place she knew she wanted to go. But, she also needed to be near Amanda now. Her best friend wouldn't fail her.

"See, I told you he wasn't right. At our age, no sex for almost six weeks means no relationship. Maybe he prefers men and can't admit it?"

"No, Amanda. What we had *was* real." Samantha blew her nose into a worn out Kleenex. "That's what was so great. No pressure, no weirdness."

"No inclination or interest or discussion of sex after that amount of time is weird. Ask anyone."

"Maybe it was me then. Maybe I wasn't sexy enough for him?"

"You're plenty sexy. Don't you think for a minute that it was you!"

They hung up the phone and Samantha began her first night of many of crying herself to sleep.

Chapter IV

*T*he coffee shop emptied out by mid-afternoon, leaving Samantha alone with her journals again. The three men who were at the table next to her finished their various drinks and went back to their office for another round of "Impress the Boss." Samantha freely admitted that not knowing where her next paycheck was coming from was still better than kissing the ass of any boss or manager or co-worker. The glass ceiling at all of the offices she ever worked in were double thick, shatter proof. As office manager, the ability to move up from her stifling position was simply not there. In most offices, if employees had no sales or other specified experience, then there were no opportunities for growth. She paid the bills and kept the office running, but each year she only received a small bonus and an even smaller raise, mostly, she realized, because she never stuck it out anywhere long enough to accrue a status of true worthiness to the company. Her last "end of the year review" was a formality and the sooner Rick dealt with her and was able to move on to the next, the better for everyone. Of course, when he emerged from his boss' office after his own review, he was aglow. None of the other employees seemed to mind him though, so she kept her mouth shut and did her job.

Now, she sat in a coffee shop, writing her novel and reading her old journals. She wasn't sure how that was going to pay the bills, but for the first time in her life, she simply didn't care. She was done caring. Done caring about men, a job, money, and happiness. She was numb and this new project of reading through her old journals was an attempt of bringing feeling back into her heart—to break through the numbness. She didn't know how or why she was doing it; she just felt that it was the place to start.

The last several pages of the first journal reflected a time in her life when she wasn't in a relationship. On one of the pages she wrote,

> *I'm tired of being alone.*
> *It's exhausting thinking about*
> *where I might meet someone, or*
> *more importantly, when.*

After reading this entry, she wrote a comment in her new journal,

> *Apparently, I'm unhappy*
> *and exhausted when I'm alone.*
> *Explore with Ragnar?*

Deciding to take a break, she went back up to the counter and ordered a hot chocolate and a sandwich. Now that the lunch crowd cleared out and she was done listening to the men chat next to her, she realized just how hungry she was.

"I'll have a hot chocolate and a toasted cheese sandwich, please," Samantha said.

"Make it provolone on sourdough with tomato." She dug into her purse for bills and coins to cover the $8.54 and handed it across the counter.

The cheese melted down the edges of the sourdough crust. A dousing of whipped cream sat atop the hot chocolate with a decadent dribbling of dark liquid chocolate on top of the white mountain of cream. By the time she walked back to her table, the pile of whipped cream had sunk into the depths of the hot chocolate and began to dissipate. Her corner spot was cozy with a large Ficus tree on one side against the wall. Works from local artists were strategically hung in places around the room. Some months displayed black and white photographs, while others showcased paintings of fruit and other tangible items usually on a display table. Samantha liked the black and white photography the best and often went from one to the next studying the subject and composition. Her taste in the photography reflected her own ability as a photographer, but the paintings reminded her of her nearly complete inability to draw or paint anything that would be recognizable. She looked around the shop as she ate her sandwich and sipped her hot chocolate. Most of the tables seated four, but there were a few two-seaters squeezed into the blend. The kitchen was behind the counter where patrons placed their orders. It was a nice place and served the purpose of escaping the four walls of her home so that she could focus on her writing and not the emptiness.

After spending another hour reading through the two selected journals, Samantha packed up and readied herself for her session with Ragnar. Now that she was launching her writing career and not tied to an office chair, she had more flexibility when scheduling her appointments with him; she could meet with him and still be home before five.

"How's the novel coming?" Ragnar asked. His pen was held tightly between two fingers and up against his chin. Samantha took her seat on the couch and sunk back into it's soft leather.

"It's going well, but I also started the project of reading through my old journals."

"Oh? And what have you discovered?"

"Actually, not much yet. It seems like I was in one of two places—in a relationship or wishing I was in a relationship. I guess that, in and of itself, is telling."

"Well, it brings up a valid point. Have you considered not focusing on being in a relationship and simply working on your book, at least until it's done?"

"No, I haven't. How could I not want love?"

"Your family and friends love you. You're loved."

"Okay, but that's freakish. I mean love with a capital 'L.'"

"Still, consider focusing on just yourself for a while. Write your book and keep that your goal. You may be surprised at what you discover." Ragnar clicked his pen. Click...click...click. Samantha wondered if he was aware that he was doing it.

"Right. I'll consider the idea."

"Have you thought about how you're going to publish your book when it's done?"

"Sure. I'll send it to a publisher or two and wait to hear from them," Samantha said.

Ragnar made a note on his notepad. Samantha was at the very least quite confident in her ability as a writer.

When she left Ragnar's office that afternoon, Samantha wondered whether or not she could go even just one day without thinking about and wanting to be in a relationship. She decided to start the next morning. If anything, the extra time will be well spent on writing and being creative, rather than sorrowful.

"You have to help me do this," Samantha told Amanda. "If I even mention the 'R' word, stop me. If I mention anyone new that I meet or want to meet, stop me."

"Okay, if you insist. Do you think it'll work?"

"I don't know, maybe. I don't even know why I'm doing this, but I agreed with Ragnar that it might be a good idea."

The next morning Samantha awoke and gathered two journals and her laptop and drove over to the coffee shop. Nestled into her corner table, she decided to alternate back and forth—one hour of working on her novel, then one hour of reading the journals. She started with the novel first, since that was supposed to be her priority, after all. Already on page 100 of it, she dove into where she left off the last time. She was tempted to go back and edit previous pages before writing more, but that stalled progress. She was more determined to finish it and then she'd be able to go back and make edits to the entire manuscript on printed paper with a good 'ol fashion red pen. Something tangible to concentrate on, let alone the feeling she'll have knowing it was completed sans editing. That time in her life was one that she looked forward to because it meant to her that she passed the first test— finishing the book.

The idea for the novel evolved one winter. She was already in her pajamas before dinner, which she ate in her bed while watching reruns of "Friends." The plot came to mind during a commercial. The idea was a story about a woman living in a cabin in the mid-west in the early 1900's whose husband had recently passed away and now was left with the farm, the cabin, and the animals. She befriends a new neighbor who hears of her situation and offers his assistance as a way to blend in with the town. Samantha hadn't determined whether or not they would marry in the actual book, or if the reader would just know that they would. Part of the conflict revolved around her two children's adjustment to their father passing and a new male figure in their lives. Quite pleased with her idea, she began writing the book in the evenings and on weekends around her work schedule. On the days when she knew Rick wouldn't be in the office, she brought the file to work so that she could work on it there.

Several months had passed before she quit her job and was able to focus on writing fulltime. She was now at the point of writing the protagonist's conflict with her children learning to accept a new male figure. This was a hard perspective to write since she didn't have children of her own and could only speculate as to how they would act, what they would feel. She contemplated their situation while she was out driving or running. Character development wasn't something she could do on paper with a pen; she had to do it in her head and usually while exercising. Something about increased endorphins helped her train of literary thought. There were times since she quit that she would wake up early and go for a run before writing because it cleared her head and allowed her to focus better.

Samantha's laptop was the best purchase she had made in the past few years. A folder titled "Writing" contained all of her short stories, poems, and the novel, *Winter's Truth*. She pulled it out and booted it up on the table. Sitting at the corner table, and while waiting for it to boot-up, she noticed a man who had walked in behind her and who was now sitting across the room. "No relationships," she reminded herself under her breath. He looked up at her, and she wondered if he could have possibly heard her. He smiled and went back to his own work. Relieved, Samantha looked down at her screen and opened up the manuscript. She was starting a new chapter and had to come up with the first line. After she had that down, the rest flowed and it was almost an hour later when she looked up again. Once again, the man was looking at her. *No!* she thought this time instead of mumbling it under her breath. *No relationships.* Then, *But he's cute and he's looking at me.* As though he telepathically received her invitation to join her, he rose from his seat and walked over to her table. *Damn! Not now. Not today. Please go away.* But the more she thought *no*, the closer he got to her table.

"Hi. What are you working on?" he asked, but didn't sit down.

"Oh this? It's a novel."

Samantha remained as nonchalant as she could.

'Really? A novel? That's funny because I'm working on a novel. A thriller actually. What genre is yours?"

"Mine? Oh, it's women's literature. I'm sure it would bore you." She added, *Now go away*, in her thoughts.

"Do you have an agent yet?" he asked, grabbing hold of the top of the chair in front of him.

"An agent? No, I haven't finished it yet," she paused then added, "Do I need an agent?"

"May I?" he asked pulling the chair away from the table.

"Uh, yeah. Sure."

"I'm Craig," he said.

"Samantha."

"Well, you'll need an agent if you plan on publishing your book. Most publishers don't look at manuscripts unless it comes from an agent. I've been sending out query letters for a few months now," Craig said.

"Query letters?" Samantha sank in her chair. She suddenly felt like she was on foreign soil and the soil was actually quick sand.

"Yes, a query. It's a letter that you send to agents to pitch your book to them with the goal of having them request the manuscript. Although they usually only take the first few chapters for review and if they like those then they'll ask for the complete script."

"Wow. I had no idea."

"It's okay. Most people don't. You have to either hear it from someone who knows or find out the hard way. Is this your first book?"

"Yes. I had the idea about a year ago and have been working on it ever since. You?"

"My first too. I've finished it and am on the third draft, so I felt comfortable sending out queries. The first three chapters are solid, so if they request those I'll feel good about sending them out."

"How'd you know where to send the letters to? What agents, I mean."

"There're plenty of ways. Reference books, internet searches, that kind of stuff. I use a spreadsheet to keep track of the ones I've contacted and their response. So far two rejections, but I'm waiting to hear back from six others before I send out another batch."

Craig went on to explain his letter, the basics of his book, and how he too quit his 9 to 5 job so that he could finish it. Stunned by his friendliness, good looks, and their similar situations, Samantha froze during most of the conversation. She chalked it up to being overwhelmed by all that she didn't know about the process of getting her book published.

When the conversation exhausted itself and he stood up to leave Craig said, "Maybe I'll see you around."

"Yeah, that'd be great," Samantha smiled as he walked away. *No relationships*, she reminded herself once again. He was too perfect anyway, she conceded, but had a hard time ignoring the tingling feeling she felt when she watched his back as he walked to his table and resumed typing.

> *Wow. I met a really great guy today. The one day I wasn't suppose to even think about relationships, this guy falls in my lap, almost literally,"* she wrote in her journal that night, cuddled up in bed. *"But, he's probably too good for me. Good looking, very confident, smart. What am I thinking? He doesn't want an unemployed wanna be writer who doesn't even know the literary field the way he does. Now I need to research query letters and agents. Yikes!*

Samantha put her journal down on her lap and twirled her pen between her fingers. He had said she needed to research agents either online or in some reference books. The task seemed daunting, another obstacle. She looked at the furniture around her room and wondered what she would sell first so that she could pay the bills when her money ran out. The dresser was only three hundred dollars new, and that was about eight years ago. Her armoire was a copy-cat of an antique. She loved it and didn't want to part with that. Finding an agent would take time, she gathered, and time wasn't something she felt she had.

Unable to sleep, Samantha brought her laptop back to bed with her, propped up against some pillows and logged onto the internet. She went to Google and performed a search on "Literary Agents" and sighed when nearly two million listings came up. The top listing seemed the best place to start, and when she clicked on that link a window to a new world opened up in front of her. Everything she read verified Craig's point—she needed an agent in order for her manuscript to reach a publisher's desk, make that an editor's desk at the publishing house.

"Okay, well how hard can this be?" She mumbled under her breath. "I'll just email them, tell 'em about my book and that'll be over with."

Even more investigation revealed to Samantha that this was going to take more work than she thought. Most of them wanted the query letter Craig mentioned, and only a few allowed e-mail submissions. Realizing that writing the query letter was her first priority, she put the laptop away and refocused on sleeping. She was too tired to do a letter to Santa Claus, let alone a letter to an agent.

This time sleep came easily, but so did the nightmares. At around two o'clock Samantha woke up from her reoccurring chilling nightmare about drowning in a vicious river. The riverbank was just out of reach and the water bubbled around her, mud and debris crushing her sides. "Saaaaaave Me!" she screamed herself awake. Pellets of sweat dripped from her forehead to her nose. Without fully understanding why, she burst into uncontrollable tears. With her head back on her favorite smooshy pillow, she pulled the stiffer one over her head as though to squelch the vigilant tears that flowed from her eyes. "I thought I didn't have any tears left!" she screamed at the Universe and anyone else who would listen. And then she fell back to sleep.

Illuminated red lights indicated the time as 8:56 a.m. "Christ!" she exclaimed as she hoped out of bed and into the shower. Ever since she was on "writer's hours" she felt that she had to spend every waking minute doing just that — writing. It was as though there was a race against the clock — her writing was the ticking hands and midnight was the completed novel. Added to that was the pressure she put upon herself to sell her book so that she could pay her bills and be satisfied with the decision she had made when she walked out of the double glass doors that day. It wasn't all about proving herself to her family or friends; it was about proving to herself that she had the muster to make her life one that she wanted, desired, and eventually — allow. Not letting the pressure surface emotionally, physically and spiritually was a daily battle.

The journals *de jour* were already stacked on her kitchen counter awaiting her when she gathered her purse and car keys.

"Why do you always work at the coffee shop?" Amanda had asked her a week earlier.

"Why? Because I can think there. Working at home just reminds me of the roof over my head I need to sustain. It's too much pressure. The coffee shop puts me more in the moment with my writing. It just works better."

"Don't all the people distract you?"

"No, not really. I can zone them out better than I can the four walls of my house."

That ended the conversation, and Samantha had to admit that Amanda's questioning where she wrote was certainly better than hearing people tell her to "find a real job."

She was well into the third journal that day, which relived the time when she met Ralph. Red hair, freckles, and soft arms were definitely not attributes she had been attracted to before, but there was something in his smile that made him work, for a while anyway. He treated her well, took her out almost every night in the beginning, and she grew to love his sense of humor. He reminded her of the Ralph on "Happy Days," but this one dressed

65

in a suit and worked at a travel agency. One night over dinner he asked her, "If you could go anywhere in the world and money wasn't an issue, where would you go?" The way he asked her was as though he would whisk her off the next day after a few key strokes on his computer.

"I dunno. Maybe Scotland. I've never been to Scotland."

"Scotland?" his face puckered as though she just hit him with a snowball. "Are you crazy? What about a warm, secluded beach somewhere in the tropics? Or Paris? Where's your flare?"

Sitting in her coffee shop hideaway, Samantha re-read the entry and wondered just where her flare was. What was wrong with Scotland? And why did everyone think beaches were the ideal travel spot? She remembered, through reading the journal and her own memory, that Ralph met someone who came into the travel agency a few weeks later and he broke up with Samantha. In hind sight, Samantha had to wonder if the lady had booked a trip to the Caribbean.

By the end of the week, Samantha had read through five journals and one thing was becoming clear. She had been miserable for five years.

"I don't get it," she told Ragnar that Thursday afternoon. "I can be fun. I can be happy. But, when I go back and read all of this all I see is how miserable I was."

"Did you see any correlations between the men? Any consistencies with how they treated you? Or you them?"

"No. They all started out okay and just ended for one reason or another. Either they met someone else or I was bored and broke up with them. No chemistry. The ones I had chemistry with were the ones who seemed to break up with me first. Robert was the worst, or at least he was the final straw before I lost it."

"How've you been about not thinking about a new relationship?"

"Well, interestingly enough, the day after we talked about that, I ended up talking to a really nice guy at the coffee shop. It was more interesting than romantic though because he was a writer too. He told me all about how I need to find an agent who will find me a publisher. I was pretty overwhelmed by this news, and all the while I was trying not to look at him as a romantic interest," Samantha said.

"Do you think he has the potential to be one?"

"I don't know. He was cute. Really smart. A writer. What more could I want? But then I went away thinking that he wouldn't want an unemployed wanna be writer?" Samantha rearranged her seating position on the couch and waited for Ragnar to answer. On some level she wanted him to say, "No it's okay. If it feels right, go with it." But he didn't give her that luxury.

"All the more reason to step back and rebuild your confidence. Give yourself time to get over Robert and to get clear about what you want," Ragnar said. "What did you learn about agents?"

Samantha explained the little bit that she had learned about agent searches and submission requirements. Ragnar admitted that he too had no idea it was that complicated. "Kinda makes sense why the industry is so tough, huh?" was what he said just before the end of their time.

That night sleep came more readily to Samantha than it had in a while. She was beyond tired and her body must have just shut down to sleep mode on its own, without the mind telling it that it needed to. She wrote three more chapters of her book in the past two days, which was great progress. The characters filled her head, talked to her while she was driving or doing dishes, and developed themselves as she wrote. They were her new colleagues and she was fine with that. Craig hadn't shown up at the coffee shop again, which made it easier to put him behind her and to refocus on her writing. Before drifting off to sleep, she thought about what Ragnar had said. That maybe she needed to give herself some more time to heal from Robert.

That had been the plan, but she still thought about him daily and still missed him. Or was it the idea of him that she missed? Either way, she felt empty and couldn't imagine how not having someone in her life could actually fill the void. It couldn't, she believed.

The dream Samantha had that night awakened her. It hadn't been scary or nightmarish, but the image and message was clear and strong. The dream started in a bright room that held only a chair where she sat. The chair was placed in the middle of the room and surrounding her, spread across the floor, were layers of journals. Each journal was opened to the middle and in big words displayed the sight that woke her up, "WRITE POSITIVE!"

"Write positive?" she uttered, half awake. *What does that mean?* This was one of the instances when Samantha decided to go back to sleep immediately, with the hopes of the dream playing itself out, of finding more answers. But, that wouldn't happen, the message was done and she awoke again hours later with the same wonderment that she had in the middle of the night. She fluffed the pillow under her head and gave herself a moment to pause and consider the dream before starting her day. She readily admitted that her previous journaling reflected all of the negative relationships she had been in, the jobs she endured under duress, and the loneliness she felt when she was between relationships. But, that was her life.

With eyes closed and lying there quietly in bed, she felt inspired to take the dream's message to a deeper level, until an idea came to her. The message in the dream was "write positive," so that was what she would do. *But why?* Of course she would need another new journal to write in. Just as she had decided to use a new one to take reflection notes on her old journals, she would buy a new one to start a "Positive Thoughts" journal. The concept was intriguing, but she decided to not share her idea with anyone, including Amanda and Ragnar. She wanted to try this experiment on her own. *What if she only wrote positively? What would happen?*

Later that morning, Samantha stood in the bookstore looking at journals and wondered about what exactly she would write. She figured the answer would come to her later, and she picked a bright yellow journal off the shelf and paid for it. She tucked it in her backpack that already held her laptop and the one last journal she had left to read. A feeling of exhilaration filled her as she left the store. The excitement about this project was a feeling she hadn't been used to, and the idea of keeping the idea private for now was that much better.

That night when she sat down to write her first entry, she felt pressured to make what she wrote just right. She didn't want to ruin it in anyway, yet she didn't know what "it" was either, other than just a feeling that she had to change her way of thinking, of writing.

> *October 27th*
>
> *This journal is specifically for writing positive thoughts. No negative thoughts will be allowed.*

There, that's a good start, she told herself then sat and waited for the next batch of words to come to her. Were they so foreign to her? Positive words? Were they not in her language? She dug deeper and summoned them.

> *I'm glad I was able to write another chapter of my book today. I love the way it's coming along, and that I'm almost finished.*

There, she did it. And, she realized, it felt good. Wanting to write more, she thought more about her day and what else she could put to paper.

> *I'm glad I quit my job. My life will be better for it. It already is better for it. Someday all of this will make sense.*

Wow, this feels good! Samantha wrote for another few minutes. It wasn't until she put the pen down that she realized she felt happy. Happy! *Maybe it's just beginner's luck*, she

71

thought, then realized it was a good thing she hadn't written that.

*****

"So, I got you a birthday present," Amanda told Samantha the next day. "When can I bring it over?"

"You know I hate celebrating my birthday," Samantha said, but was silently happy about the idea of receiving a gift and that she was remembered. "But, all right. How 'bout we go out to eat? We can do Thai," Samantha suggested, wanting to make an evening of it.

"Can't. Have to bring it to your house, and don't ask why. I'll be there at six with Thai food and your present in tow. How's that?"

"Okay, see you then."

By five thirty Samantha was getting as anxious as she was curious about her present. There had been birthdays when she had a boyfriend who gave her gifts—some were from Victoria's Secret, others were the type you'd give a friend. None blew her away. Looking around the kitchen, she realized there were dishes in the sink and bills on the counter. Neither of which she wanted to look at, so she spent the half hour before Amanda arrived cleaning them up and before she knew it, there was a knock at her door. She dried her hands and hung the dish towel back in its spot. As she approached the door, she heard a ruffling on the front porch of her cabin, peaking her curiosity. On the other side of the door stood Amanda with a big smile on her face.

"Stay right there; don't take another step!" Amanda instructed once inside.

"Okay," Samantha said, looking at the large unwrapped cardboard box on the floor. Amanda disappeared back outside and around the corner of the cottage. When she returned, she was followed by a bouncing, black puppy.

"Oh, Amanda! What did you do?"

"Meet your birthday present! It's a girl!"

"Oh...my...God! She's adorable!" Samantha bent down and greeted the puppy, who leapt into her lap, licked her face, and spun its tail wildly.

"I think she likes you," Amanda knelt down. "She was in a litter of pups that my boss' dog had a few months ago."

"I really appreciate the sentiment, but I can't have a puppy! I can barely take care of myself right now, what am I going to do with her?"

"You're going to raise her, that's what you're going to do with her. She's going to love you, and unlike all those stupid men, she won't leave you. You'll see; it'll work out fine." Amanda reached over and grabbed the box. "I took the liberty of picking up a few things to start you out. There's a leash..."

"Wait, wait, wait. I don't know about this." Samantha stood up and closed her eyes and tilted her head to the sky. "This is a big responsibility."

"Give it time. Please?"

Samantha looked down and watched the puppy sniff the nearby azalea bush. "She is cute," she admitted and let out a deep sigh.

"Yay! So, you'll keep her?"

"All right, I'll give it a try. But no promises," Samantha said with as much sternness as she could muster.

Pleased with the compromise, Amanda went to her car and pulled out the Thai food she promised and the rest of the puppy supplies she splurged on. Samantha walked the puppy around her yard and introduced it to all of the bushes before they met Amanda in the kitchen for dinner.

"So, what're you gonna name her?"

Samantha hadn't begun to think about a name. The puppy was barely inside the house. "I dunno. I'll have to think about it."

"No queer names just because she's black, like Midnight or Blackie."

"I wouldn't do that to her. I need to spend time with her before I can name her."

"Okay, but don't take too long. She'll need to know when you're calling her."

After dinner they set up the puppy's dog bed, put her collar on—a bright yellow one—and watched as the pup dug around her new bed, circled a few times, lay down and fell sound asleep.

"Awww, look at her," Samantha said.

"You'll be thanking me for this for years to come," Amanda told Samantha, then gathered her things to leave.

"Right, right. Okay, I'll be thanking you. We'll see." Samantha shut the door behind Amanda, shook her head, and went back to the living room where the puppy was sleeping. "Good Lord, what am I suppose to do with you?" she whispered, but no answer came.

When Samantha went to bed, she pulled out her Positive Thoughts journal and wrote that she was indeed thankful for friends like Amanda and even for the puppy, as she was sure it would work out one way or another. Since it was her birthday, she decided to write a wish list for the coming year.

October 28th

My Birthday Wishes (I am entitled to more than one, aren't I?): that I sell my novel, which means that I also wish I find a great agent. My advance money will be sufficient to cover my expenses while I write my second novel. I meet (when I'm ready) a really great guy. The guy. The one. One that I want to spend the rest of my life with and one who wants to spend the rest of his life with me. I wish that the puppy learns to sleep through the night quickly! I'll stop

*there because I know those are all
tall orders.* ☺

She began the habit of signing her journal entries with a smiley face. After closing the journal, she placed it on her night table and spent a minute envisioning all that she had wished for before blowing out the candle next to her bed.

Chapter V

*T*he clock displayed 3:30 a.m. in a glowing red. The sound bellowing from the living room was the puppy crying. Samantha hurled herself out of bed and ran downstairs to her. "Owww!" she cried as she stubbed her toe on the doorframe. "What's the matter pup? Do you need to go out?" There were a few things that Samantha knew about raising a puppy and one of them was that they needed to go out often. The puppy sat there looking at Samantha from her bed, which for now was inside the large cardboard box. When Samantha looked around there were no accidents. "Okay, let's get you out." The cold air was a stark contrast to the warm bed Samantha left behind minutes ago. The puppy scurried across the grass and found a place to relieve herself. Not even the bright porch light was enough to spot her in the dark of night, but it was only a moment later before she bounded back to Samantha's feet. "Good girl!" Samantha told her and picked her up to cuddle her.

When they got back inside, the puppy wiggled her way out of Samantha's arms, dropping to the ground just as Samantha leaned over. "Careful little girl. That's a long drop."

Samantha watched as the puppy ran across the room and grabbed a plush toy from the corner. "No, it's not play time; it's back to bed time," and back into the box the puppy went with one swoop from Samantha's arms to the bed. "You go back to sleep, ya hear?" The puppy looked at her, but clearly didn't comprehend. The whining started and Samantha knew it was going to be a long night. By five-thirty the puppy was in bed with her. "Now will you sleep?" She did and the two of them didn't wake up again until eight-fifteen.

By the time Samantha took care of the puppy, went through her own morning rituals, and made it to the coffee shop to work, it was approaching ten o'clock. Her usual corner table was taken by a college student—she surmised by the sprawl of textbooks, so she settled for an alternative table, wondering if the change would throw off her writing rhythm. She had developed a ritual over the past several weeks.

While unpacking her laptop, she thought about the chapter ahead of her. She had finished an intense chapter the last time she was there and looked forward to delving into the next one.

"How's the novel coming along?" a voice asked from behind. She turned around to find Craig facing her.

"God, you scared me," Samantha said. She immediately calmed down though. "It's good. Hit a peak scene yesterday, so today I'm writing the aftermath of it."

"Great." He smiled warmly at her. "Did you take some time to look up agents? I'm sure there are a bunch who handle women's lit."

"A little bit. It's pretty overwhelming seeing all of those names and what they require. I've also been thinking about my query letter, but haven't written it yet."

"Just make sure it starts off grabbing their attention. Business format, but the writing needs to have literary flare to stand out against all of the doldrums. Yours needs to POP!"

"Pop?"

"You know, stand out and make the agent say, 'Yes! Finally someone good.' Some of them see hundreds of letters a day and it's the writing that makes you stand out, not flowery letter head and all that garbage."

"Boy, you really know your stuff." Samantha put her chin in the palm of her hand. She didn't want the conversation to end.

"Well, we'll see. I'm just starting out too, but I've done my research." Craig was taking the table next to her and turned for a minute to put his things down. He carried a backpack that had a slot for a laptop. When he pulled it out, he said, "Here, take a look at my query letter. Different genre, but the format and concepts are the same."

79

Samantha stood up, leaned against a chair and watched while it booted up and he opened the document. After she read his letter, she said, "Geez, that's good. I guess I need to start on one."

"How far along are you with your book?"

"About four chapters to go. I'm not convinced I love the ending I have in my head, so that could change and require another chapter. Won't know till I write it."

"You could start drafting the letter in the meantime, especially if you need a break from the book." Craig sat down in a chair at his table and pulled his laptop closer to him. "I have a spreadsheet that tracks all of the agents. Last week one of them asked for the first three chapters of my book, so I sent that off. I was so psyched."

"That's great!" Samantha said.

"Well, it's the next step. They'll want the full manuscript if they like the sample chapters. It's a long process."

Samantha let go of the chair she had been gripping and sat back down in the chair at her table.

"That's what I'm afraid of," she said.

They smiled at one another and then let the other go back to work on their books. Nearly two hours passed before she looked up again. She hadn't been that engrossed in her work in several days and the thought crossed her mind that she was being pulled along through osmosis with Craig. She looked over at him while he was busy typing away. For the first time, she was able to take a good, uninterrupted look at him. Every other time she had been so absorbed in what he was telling her about agents and publishing, and worrying about her own situation. He seemed to be eons ahead of her, and there she thought she had been on the brink of making it to the New York Times Best Seller List. *How could she have been so naïve?*

Looking at Craig she wondered how he knew to do all of this footwork; who told him? She pacified her insecurity by realizing that he had to learn it somehow or somewhere too. As she thought about it, she noticed his dark curly hair. It was just long enough that the temptation to run her fingers through it was strong, if anything just to feel the curls between her sinewy fingers. He had nice ears, they weren't too small the way Ralph's had been, nor did they stick out too much the way Peter's had. No, his were nice. A rugged jaw line accented his wide mouth structure, but he wasn't smiling so she couldn't notice his teeth. Deep brown irises centered nicely in the whites of his eyes. And it was then that she realized how good looking he was and that she was treading in deep water where she may not be able to swim.

"No dating until you're ready," Ragnar's words settled into her head, reminding her that she wasn't suppose to be looking at men as dating potential. Ragnar was right; she had to take a break. Before Craig had the chance to notice she was looking at him, she stood up and went to order lunch at the counter—her usual cheese sandwich and an ice tea.

"That looks good. Traditional grilled cheese?" Craig asked when Samantha returned to her table.

"Kinda traditional. I order provolone on sour dough with tomato. Not what a kid would like, so I guess it's an adult version of a childhood favorite," Samantha explained. *Shut up*, she thought, *that was way too much information over just a sandwich.*

"Well, it looks good."

Samantha sat down with her lunch and re-read what she had written that morning. Happy with what she read, she only made a few edits before continuing on with the rest of the chapter. By two o'clock she knew she had to go home and let the puppy out, but since she was on a roll, she wanted to come back to the coffee shop and finish.

"Are you going to be here for about a half hour?" she asked Craig.

"Yeah, I'll be here till at least five. I'm at a critical point and don't want to stop."

"Me neither, but my friend just gave me a puppy for my birthday. I've gotta go home and let her out real quick."

"A puppy? What kind?"

"She's a black lab, mostly. Really cute, but not much bladder control right now." *Did she just say the word bladder to him?*

"Gotcha, sure, I'll watch your stuff."

Samantha didn't know why she trusted him, but she did and left everything but her wallet and car keys behind.

When she walked into her house, the puppy was so excited to see her that she almost didn't make it outside before peeing.

"Good girl!" Samantha told her and scooped her back up. "I'm sorry I'm not here much today, but we'll play later. Deal?"

Samantha took the lick to her face as an agreement in puppy talk. Back on the ground, the puppy ran around sniffing. Samantha ran alongside her, hoping to tire her out for the afternoon. They did two laps around the house before Samantha put the puppy back in the dog bed in the box where she fell back to sleep. Samantha had already learned how hard the puppy would play and how hard the puppy would sleep. There was no middle ground.

The drive back to the coffee shop was unnerving. Part of the way Samantha was behind a school bus making its rounds, and once in town she managed to hit every red light. Her promise to be back in a half an hour was squelched, and it was closer to an hour before she walked back into the shop. Sitting at her table, nose to the laptop screen was Craig.

"What're you doing?" Samantha asked.

"Your computer was beeping because the battery was dying, so I plugged it in for you. Then the title of your book caught my eye, and I started to read it. You're good. You're writing, I mean, it's good."

Samantha didn't know whether to be flattered or angered for the intrusion of her privacy, even though she left her things in his care. Unable to answer, she just stood there.

"Sorry. I shouldn't have. But, you are a good writer." Craig smiled at her and stood up out of the seat. Samantha looked at his soft eyes and fought the melting of her heart, her stomach, her legs. Damn.

"It's okay. I was just surprised that a man would want to read any type of women's lit." *Good recovery,* she thought.

"Well, it caught my attention. Your character development is nicely done. Not that I read all that much to know. But, I'd focus your query letter on her innate insecurities. I'm guessing she'll overcome those?"

"Yes, she does. I'll think about that for the query. Thanks," Samantha put her wallet and keys down and retook her seat. The compliment was reassuring. She hadn't shared the book with anyone yet, not even Amanda. But, sometimes a stranger's opinion is best because it's not biased.

The positive entries were piling up in her journal, and that night, with the puppy under one arm sound asleep, Samantha added another entry,

November 4th

I was able to write quite a bit of Winter's Truth today. It felt good to get over the climatic point of the novel and down the slope toward the ending. Craig gave me positive feedback on it, which was reassuring and helpful. Tomorrow I'm going to focus on my query letter. Yikes! (In a good way.) ☺

It was after writing this entry when Samantha had the idea to not only write about good things that happened to her, but also the good things she *wanted* to happen. She turned to the next blank page and wrote:

November 11th

Dear Samantha,

We were intrigued by your query letter. Please send us the first fifty pages of your manuscript for our review.

Then she wrote:

December 12th

Dear Samantha,

As we anticipated, we loved the start of the book. Please send the full manuscript.

Then

January 19th
Dear Samantha,
We would like to sign you
as a client. Please contact our
offices   at   your   earliest
convenience.

She finished, closed her journal and placed the pen on top of it. She smiled, taking in all of the emotion of how it would feel to have those letters sent to her. It made her feel good, feel right with her world, to have written not only positive events that were already happening, but the dreams she had for her future as well. And that was the purpose of this journal, she thought.

The next few days Samantha initiated a routine between writing at the coffee shop, letting the puppy out, and then more writing. By the time Thursday rolled around, she realized that she was thankful for the session with Ragnar. It seemed that, other than a few interactions with Craig and a handful of phone calls from Amanda checking on the puppy, she realized that she really hadn't carried a conversation with anyone and that she had been too busy to notice. As she sat in Ragnar's office waiting for him to take his seat across from her, Samantha had an epiphany. "Ragnar, I just realized that I didn't feel lonely once this week."

"Really? Boy, that's progress." Ragnar sat down and put his pen to his pad, scribbling what Samantha imagined had to do with the comment she just made.

"I was so busy all week that I didn't have much time to think about it. Amanda gave me a puppy for my birthday. That's been a lot of work."

"Wow, a puppy? That's a big present and commitment."

"I know. At first I didn't want her, but she's really cute and it's working out. I'll admit she gives me a purpose that I didn't have before."

Samantha then went on to describe her conversations with Craig, but kept it to their discussions about writing and finding an agent. He listened as she spoke, wrote down notes intermittently, and seemed genuinely happy that she had a new friend. Samantha went as far as to tell Ragnar that Craig complimented her novel, and that it was her first outside acknowledgement of her writing abilities. That was huge for her.

What she didn't tell Ragnar about was the Positive Journal she started. She wasn't ready to tell anyone about it yet. She just wanted to see how, or if, things would unfold. It had been almost a month since she started it and she had to admit she felt better, but wasn't sure if that was because of the puppy, the progress with her book, talking to Craig, or just because she was in a good place for a change. She didn't want to jinx it by talking about it, not even with Ragnar.

When Samantha returned home after their session, the greeting she received from the puppy was more than welcoming. She laughed at the bouncing pup that lurched at her feet when she walked in the door. Samantha immediately let the puppy outside and watched as it ran around sniffing everything her nose found. The weather had been unusually warm that day considering winter was fast approaching. A rope hammock hung between two trees in the back yard, and Samantha brushed the leaves off of it and sat down, swinging gently with her face toward the sun. The puppy ran about the back yard, keeping itself busy with all that nature had to offer.

"We need to name you, little girl. It's been way too long." Ignoring her, the puppy scattered about. "Fine, I'll come up with something myself, you lunatic." *That's it!* "Lunar! That's what I'll call you. Lunar. How's that?" No answer, but the name was settled.

Amanda agreed the name was fitting and far enough off the usual track of names for jet-black puppies. "That's perfect since it's a full moon tonight, too!" Amanda said. A fact that Samantha hadn't realized, but it reassured her that she came up with the ideal name for her pup. They agreed to take the puppy to the dog park the next day and when Samantha pulled out her Positive Journal before going to bed, she made note of Lunar's name.

I named Lunar today. What a perfect name for her. I'll try to not call her 'Lunatic' too often. Or 'Looney.' Also, I wrote my query letter the other day and showed it to Craig. He said it was good, so I sent it out to a handful of agents. I'm excited about hearing back from them with good news.

She caught herself before she wrote "whether they like it or not." Through her positive writing, she began to catch every thought that had any negative connotation and rearranged her thoughts to reflect completely positive ones before putting them to paper.

When an agent takes me on, I'm sure they will find a publisher who will be the perfect fit for my novel.

Samantha was initially amazed at how difficult and rigid it felt to force positive thoughts for this journal, but over time the end result was that it felt good to eventually put the words of encouragement and gratitude on paper. Eventually, the pages were filled with ideas such as publishing her book, finding an agent, having her expenses covered while she continued to write, and eventually finding the man of her dreams when the time was right.

She knew she was asking for a lot, but there were people out there who had these things. She thought, *If they can have these things, why can't I? I deserve it too.*

Giving herself permission, she realized, was a big step and quite possibly the first and most important step toward achieving goals. In thinking about the people she knew who had what they wanted in life, things they had at one time desired, it dawned on her that they all gave themselves — whether consciously or not — allowing themselves to have it. By doing so, they literally drew their desires to them. With this knowledge in mind, Samantha made a new pact with herself. Besides writing in her Positive Journal, she would, during the day and evenings, think in a way that allowed her to have what seemed unattainable. In that moment, a rush came over her, as though her spirit had been jolted awake. She was driving home as these thoughts came to her and she took the time to pull over to the side of the road so that she could fully absorb them.

"Maybe that's the secret? Maybe I need to not only think that I want a certain life, but believe wholeheartedly that I deserve it." Samantha didn't talk out loud to herself very often, but in this case it was as though she needed to hear the words, not just think them. Again, her spirit joyfully soared throughout her body and a level of happiness that she had never experienced swarmed her body. Had she not known better, she would have thought she was delusional. Cars continued to pass her by as she parked alongside the road, immersed in her new reality. She wanted to hang on to this emotion, this elation, for as long as she could because it was powerful and it drove her to wanting more from her life and believing, more importantly, that she deserved it.

*****

On the way to the coffee shop, Samantha stopped at a bookstore to pick up a guide to literary agents, a book Craig recommended she buy. When she walked through the door, an employee was stocking the display in the window. *One day my book will be there*, she thought. Then, *Wow, did I just think that? Yes, I did. And yes, I'm right. My book will be there*, she thought. The employee looked up at her and smiled as though he read her mind. "Can I help you?"

Samantha told him what she was looking for and was led to the aisle where the guide was shelved. She was surprised at how thick it was and initially found it intimidating, but she corrected that thought by acknowledging the flow of information that would come from reading it. This was a book packed with the information she needed to further her career as a writer. This was powerful stuff!

As she rang up Samantha's book, the woman at the register grinned and asked, "Are you a writer?"

"Yes, I am," Samantha proudly responded. The power behind saying those words was freakishly exciting. The woman handed Samantha her receipt and told her to have a great day.

The coffee shop was busy, but Samantha was able to grab her usual seat and that morning she finished her novel. She would still have to print it and go through it with a red pen, but when she wrote the last word of the last chapter, she leaned back in the chair, wrapped her hands behind her head and sighed a pleasing sigh.

"Done," she said.

"Finished?" The voice was Craig's.

"Oh, hi. Yup, done! Of course I still need to attack it with the red pen, but boy it feels good to finish the first draft."

"Well then, a celebratory drink is in order. What's your choice?"

"Hot chocolate...skim with whipped cream. Thanks!"

"Coming right up!" Craig left to order their drinks and Samantha looked back down at her computer screen. She was really finished. When Craig returned, he took a seat next to her and asked her how it felt to be a novelist.

"A novelist? Yeah, I guess I am. It feels great," she licked the whipped cream off her lip. Craig reached over with his finger and wiped a spot that she missed.

"Got it," he said. Embarrassed, Samantha licked her lips again to assure that he wouldn't need to wipe more away.

"So, how's your book coming along?" she asked.

"Good. I'm on the second round of edits. Oh, and guess what? Another agent requested the first fifty pages!"

"That's awesome! Interesting that they asked for a specific number of pages rather than just chapters."

"Honestly, they usually know within a few pages whether or not they're going to take you on. But, if the first few pages keep them reading, they like to have ample work to evaluate. They're all different though. Some want chapters and some want a certain number of pages. Just depends." Craig lifted his cup in a toast to Samantha for finishing her novel. "To you. You'll see, it'll all start falling into place. Timing has a role in it too."

"Timing is an excuse if you ask me," Samantha said.

"An excuse?"

"Yeah, it's a cop-out from the universe to not give you what you want when you want it."

"Oh, no no, dear. It's meant to give you time in between to process what you had and prepare for what's coming down the pipe. It's all good," Craig said, but Samantha lost him at "dear." She thought for a moment and let the rest of his words sink in. Could it be that she was in a time of healing? What would come at the end of that time? She surmised that worrying about it wasn't the answer; that letting the universe show you was all you could really do, but she wasn't completely convinced that if something else didn't come along sooner, that it would at least help with the healing.

"Right, time for processing between events. Got it. Still a cop out. What if the next best thing helps you get over the last one?"

"Then it would just be a Band-Aid. Not the real deal and it would falter. You'll see. When you sell your book you'll know it was the right time. Trust me on that at least," Craig winked at her and squeezed her hand. A strong passion flowed through her when his skin touched hers. *What was that?* She asked herself. *No dating, no dating.*

Samantha used the excuse that she had to let Lunar out and began to pack up her belongings. Craig seemed unaware that his actions struck her the way they had, and excused himself from the table, telling her to have a great afternoon and gave her another congratulations.

On the way home Samantha realized she hadn't thought about Robert all day, and in fact, over the past several days his name came to mind only on occasion and only when she had a quiet moment. Was she finally getting over him? Was she freeing herself from his mental and emotional imprisonment? She told herself, yes, and continued down the road.

***

"What do you mean you got up and left?" Amanda screeched into the phone.

"Well, what was I supposed to do? I'm not dating. I don't want to date right now."

"Okay, so now that Mr. Wonderfully Right comes along, you're going to blow him off because Ragnar told you to take time to yourself? What's that about?"

"It's me learning to be okay with being alone." Samantha discovered over the past month that she had grown used to being alone and that she actually enjoyed her new solo routine.

"Whatever. I just don't want you to become one of those old maids."

"Hey, when you find Mr. Right, you can talk all you want about it," Samantha rebutted. Amanda hadn't wanted to be in a relationship by choice for several years after being stilted at the alter when she was twenty-five years old. Ron was the one she thought she'd spend the rest of her life with, and the experience left her cold to relationships and absorbed in her work. There was an occasional dinner, mostly set up by friends, but nothing more than that in three years. It was her choice, and Samantha laid off the subject a long time ago. Unless, of course,

Amanda pushed the dating issue too far with Samantha; then it was fair game.

"Just looking out for you, hun. You're exactly right; I don't want to see you old and bitter like me."

Lunar was curled up at Samantha's feet chewing on a rope toy that Amanda brought over a few days before. Samantha wondered if Amanda wasn't living vicariously through her at times, although she couldn't image why she'd want to. Her life was calmer now, but not one to envy per se.

> *I'm glad I'm at least willing to take chances to be loved. I wish Amanda would meet someone and be willing to take the leap too. I believe I can love again, and I believe I can be loved. I believe that I will find an agent to sign my book with and that it will sell. I believe. I have to believe.*

The last words were difficult to write while summonsing the actual feeling that she really/truly believed them. She consciously recognized that what she was writing in her Positive Journal was harder to follow through with in reality. Yet, she knew it would take time to align what she was writing with what she was truly thinking and feeling. After a period of time though, and with a new calmness in her life, she found it easier to connect her written word to her thoughts. With each passing day, the process became a habit, and then it became normal.

Lunar rolled over on her back, exposing her three month old belly to the ceiling and let out a puppy yawn that drew a smile to Samantha's face.

"C'mon little Lunar, let's get you out once more before bedtime."

After letting her out for a few minutes, Lunar ran back into the house where Samantha stood in the doorway waiting for her and jumped back up on the bed where she nested and settled in for the night. It had been over a week since Lunar slept in her own bed. Samantha loved the company and warmth the puppy provided and felt bad leaving her in the dog bed all day and again all night. It allowed them to bond, and when they were outside, Lunar bounced and played, but always kept Samantha in sight. Knowing that puppies needed routine, Samantha was at least able to provide that for Lunar, and in turn for herself. The combination gave meaning to her daily routine.

Chapter VI

*O*n most days Samantha's mailbox was filled with junk mail and a bill or two. Although, since she started sending out query letters to agents, a system she worked into her routine, she started receiving self addressed stamped envelopes. Craig had prepared her for being able to accept the rejections and not to take them personally, which didn't come easily with her overall history. But, with each rejection she folded the letter back up, stuck it in a big envelope with the others, logged the response in her spreadsheet and said, "Well, you're just not the agent for me. Someone better will come along." At first, just like the Positive Journal writing, it sounded phony to her, but after a dozen rejections rolled in, she acclimated to those words too.

It was a Thursday and she was home for lunch to let Lunar out before a session with Ragnar. She was looking forward to seeing him, as she had lots of good things to share. It seemed that more and more she was sharing good news with him rather than crying on his proverbial shoulder. Amanda suggested Samantha take a break from the sessions, but being superstitious and not wanting to mess things up while they were going well, Samantha continued. Ragnar had reduced his fee for her when she quit her job and lost her medical insurance, which made it doable to continue.

The dishes were neatly stored in the dishwasher, which she would run that night; the bed was made, another habit she developed each morning; and the living room was free of clutter...mostly to keep it puppy-safe.

"Lunar, c'mon let's get the mail before I have to leave," Samantha called from the hallway. From down the hall came the patter of four paws, each one trying to keep up with the next, stumbling over each other and causing her to nearly miss the turn.

"Good girl!"

The walk to the mailbox wasn't long, but the gravel driveway gave prudence to Lunar's paws, which continued to stumble over one another. Her efforts to keep up with her master were endearing. One day she'd fill out those paws and would be ahead of Samantha.

Sitting inside the mailbox were four pieces of mail: one from a car dealership advertising yet another special on interest rates, one was a post card from a church having a rummage sale that weekend, one was her phone bill, and the bottom one was a self addressed stamped envelope that she was now accustom to receiving.

"Lunar, if they want me, they would call or e-mail, right? Only rejections come in these envelopes, and I'm in too good of a mood to read a rejection right now."

Lunar followed Samantha back to the house and inside where Samantha went to her bathroom to touch up her make-up and run a brush through her hair. When she returned to the living room, Lunar was spitting out a piece of paper.

"Loony girl, what did you get?" Samantha squatted down and pulled the paper out of Lunar's mouth; the words on top of the page that emerged made Samantha fall backwards onto the floor.

"Dear Ms. Sounder, We were quite impressed with your query and the scope of your work. Please send to us the first three chapters of *Winter's Truth* for further evaluation."

The rest of the words were formalities.

"Lunar! Did you see that? No, of course you didn't, you were too busy chewing it. They want my chapters! They want my chapters!"

By now Samantha was jumping up and down in the living room, waving the letter in the air.

"Oh My God! I've got to print the chapters. No, wait, I need to calm down. If I hurry, I'll mess up. I don't want to mess up."

Lunar sat looking up at Samantha with ears perked and head cocked. Her tail wagged gently as though she wasn't sure if Samantha had gone crazy or whether what she was saying was good news for a puppy.

A rush ran through Samantha as she looked at her watch and discovered she had twenty minutes to make it to Ragnar's office. She plopped Lunar in her bed in the box, grabbed her car keys, and sped down the driveway with a trail of gravel kicking out behind her.

"Sorry I'm a bit late, Ragnar," Samantha breathed as she rushed through his door. "But, I've got exciting news!"

"Oh, what's that?" Ragnar asked.

Samantha had a sudden thought of wondering if telling him would jinx it.

"Um," she started, "I've been doing great. I feel really good about life right now. So, how are you?"

Ragnar gleaned at her over his glasses. She could tell he wasn't falling for the generalization, but he let it slide.

"What's been happening?" he asked.

"Can't put my finger on it. I just feel good about things. Amanda thinks an alien captured the old me and replaced me with a new, content version of myself. She also accused me of being in love! Can you imagine that?"

"Are you?"

"What? In love? No. Why can't people believe I can just be happy?"

"Oh, I believe you can be. Just thought I'd double check. Have you seen Craig?"

"Yes, but I'm not in love. We're writing buddies. I've learned a bunch from him about finding an agent." It was now that Samantha wanted to divulge her good news to take the conversation off of Craig and to prove that she had her own personal reasons to be happy, but she refrained.

As soon as she left Ragnar's, Samantha slipped over to the coffee shop. Craig was the only one she wanted to tell about the agent because she knew he'd understand and would be excited and not skeptical of her news. Inside the shop, it was quiet, and as she suspected, he was sitting at his regular table. "Guess what?" It was her turn to sneak up on him.

"What," he asked, looking up at her with an ear to ear grin—one that she forced herself to ignore, especially when she had good news to tell.

"An agent wants my partial!" One thing she had learned from Craig was the literary lingo she had been lacking.

"You're kidding me? That's great!"…And there was the genuine happiness Samantha had hoped for. She knew Amanda and Ragnar would be happy for her, but it just wouldn't be the same as telling another writer; it was as though they were in their own fraternity.

"I'm so excited. Even if it doesn't come to fruition, at least someone wanted to see more of my work," she beamed.

"That's it. That's the attitude you have to take. Did you mail it out yet?"

"No, I just got the letter in the mail today. I'll print the chapters tonight and mail them out tomorrow."

"Make sure your cover letter doesn't have any typos, and it helps to write 'Requested Material' on the package so it doesn't get thrown in the slush pile."

"Wow, good point. I wouldn't have thought of that."

"Tricks you learn along the way. Most agents will remind you to note the requested material too." Craig leaned back in his chair and clasped his hands behind his head. "So, welcome to the big times, Samantha. Have a seat if you want to take a load off."

"No, I don't think I can sit still! Plus, I've gotta go home and start printing. I'll be here tomorrow though. I want to start outlining a new book. The idea came to me yesterday."

"Ah, that's the best approach. Move on to another project and let this one go to the agents. You'll see."

He had a point, and Samantha was looking forward to starting a new book now that her first one was finished. Deciding to alternate between editing *Winter's Truth* and writing her new book, *Fresh Fruit and Fresh Men*, seemed like a good balance. *Winter's Truth* had been a dark women's literature novel, but *Fresh Fruit* was going to be lighter. Not quite chick-lit, but a lighter women's-lit book.

On the way home Samantha stopped and picked up a few groceries and while putting them away, her phone rang. She let it go to voicemail since her hands were full. After her outgoing message finished, the voice through the machine said, "Hey, it's me! Where are you?"

Amanda. Not sure if Samantha could handle keeping the agent secret from her, Samantha didn't pick up the phone. She would call Amanda back tomorrow when she was settled down and her emotions were in better control.

Her office was the smaller of the bedrooms and was rarely used since she had the laptop and worked at the coffee shop. But, the printer was stocked with paper and ink, awaiting its purpose. The first three chapters totaled forty-two pages. She double checked the header to make sure it accurately displayed her name, the manuscript name, and the page numbers. A tip Craig had told her. The cover page displayed her full name, address, phone number, e-mail, the approximate word count and the genre. The title was in capital letters in the middle of the page. She loved how official it looked. From the agent's envelope, she copied the name and address and printed a mailing label. While waiting for the manuscript pages to print, she wrote the cover letter.

"Dear Ms. Jackson, Thank you for your interest,"

Ugh. Too typical. Be original, she thought. After typing and deleting several words, Samantha was finally satisfied that her cover letter was perfect. She packaged it together with the first three chapters and put them in a manila envelope. The agent's label was placed with care in the middle of the envelope and Samantha's return address adhered to the top left corner. She stuck another self addressed stamped envelope in the manila envelope before sealing it all together.

"Lunar, there it is ready to go," she said, looking down at the pup who was sitting by her chair, waiting patiently for her last walk of the night.

*****

Winter set in overnight. The next morning the fading green grass was tinted with a white haze of frost. Lunar didn't seem to mind the cold beneath her paws as she found her favorite spot in the yard to pee. Samantha stood in the door with a heavy fleece robe wrapped tightly around her. The cold air caught her breath and froze it in midair. A kettle of hot water began to stir and bubble on the stove, the whistle wasn't long off.

"C'mon, Lunar. It's cold out here."

Back inside Lunar ate her breakfast as she did every morning — as though she hadn't been fed since she stepped her paws in the house a few months ago. Growing puppies, Samantha learned, slept, ate, and played in equal amounts. The envelope addressed to Ms. Jackson sat on the kitchen counter next to her purse. The post office didn't open until eight thirty, and it was only seven thirty, so she took the time to make her tea, eat a bowl of oatmeal, clean the kitchen, and straighten up the house before leaving. By eight twenty-five, she was at the door, kissing Lunar on her head, and saying good-bye.

"I'll be back after lunch. You be a good girl," she said.

"First class mail, please," Samantha instructed the clerk at the post office. Her internal thoughts continued, *and don't lose this. My life's dream is in that package. Do you have any idea what would happen if you guys lose this package? That would simply ruin my life.* Her hands trembled as she pulled a five dollar bill out of her wallet and handed it to the clerk, "Too much coffee already," she lied to the woman, not wanting the her to know just how precious the package was despite its lifeless exterior. Samantha didn't want them knowing that they were in control of delivering her manuscript on a proverbial silver platter to Ms.

Jackson. *That would be too much pressure on them*, she thought.

Her drive to the coffee shop allowed her time to settle and to refocus her attention on her next book. Not a huge proponent of outlines and charts before starting a book, she preferred to dive in after hours of thought.

"Good morning," Craig was already at the shop and deep into his revisions. "Sleep in a little late today?"

"No, smarty, I was mailing my script off to the agent, Ms. Jackson."

"Oh, that's right. How'd that all go?"

"Fine, if you don't count my wanting to lecture the postal clerk as to how to handle it with delicate gloves. Not that it's not on some conveyor belt right now, or bundled in a big bin with a thousand other packages. Daunting, isn't it?"

"Ah, no worries. It's their job. Your goods will be fine. Just focus on your next book while you wait. Beats stressing and worrying about what you can't control."

"So, just how many self-help books did you read before you were able to lighten up?"

"About ten," he laughed. "No, really, I've learned as I've gone along. The road of hard knocks eventually smoothes itself out and when your wheels glide along the sleek pavement, the momentum builds and there's no stopping. You'll see. It happens if you let it." Craig pushed his laptop case aside. "Do you want to sit here and work?"

Samantha looked down at the table that should normally seat four, but writers took up a lot of space with their laptops, bags, manuscripts, and the need for elbow room to think. "No, that's okay. I'll sit over there. I don't want to distract you."

Craig nodded at her, "It's a writer thing, I know." Relieved that he understood it wasn't about the physical space, but about the mental space. Samantha settled in at her own table and threw herself into her next book.

Happy with the dozen or so pages she wrote that morning, Samantha sat up straight and stretched. She tried to make a conscious effort to stop and stretch while working. The idea of being completely hunched over for hours on end and what it would lead to later in life made her cringe. She glanced around the coffee shop and noted all the people in groups eating lunch.

Thanksgiving was coming up and she hadn't made any plans for the four day weekend. For the first time in her life, she wasn't concerned about having someone to share it with, or whose house she'd be going to—her boyfriend's family or her own. The simplicity of her life, the lack of emotional clutter, had become a mindset she never imagined she'd be content with. Lunar helped, made her laugh. Her writing was her escape, and Craig provided peripheral companionship and understanding. Amanda and Ragnar were her bouncing boards. Everything was in place.

"Sorry to bother you. I know you're up to your chin in characters and plots, but I wanted to run something by you," Craig said. He stood behind the chair on the other side of her table. He leaned inward, gripping the back of the chair for support. *Uh oh*, Samantha thought. She didn't say anything, though, leaving Craig to figure out that he could continue. "The film festival is showing 'A Street Car Named Desire' tomorrow night. Thought you'd like to see some Tennessee Williams literature on screen?"

"As in a date?" Samantha shocked herself by saying the "D" word.

"Well, it doesn't need to be if you don't want to. We can just go. But,"

"No, no, that's okay. We can go." Samantha cut him off before he backed out of the prospect of it being a date.

"Great. It starts at seven. We can grab a bite to eat before hand if you want. Some place other than here?"

"Sure. That sounds fine. You pick, I'll eat anything." *Great*, she thought, *now I sound like a pig who'll eat whatever's put in front of her*.

"There's a good Thai restaurant right by the theater," Craig said, releasing his grip from the chair. "Does that sound good?"

"Yes, it does. I'll meet you there around six?" Samantha's words weren't keeping up with her mind and when Craig nodded in agreement, smiled and left saying he had some errands to run, she sat motionless in her chair in the coffee shop with her novel in front of her, letting the idea that she just made a date, set in.

"Finally!" Amanda screeched into the phone later that afternoon. Samantha called her when she went home to let Lunar out. "Look, I've got a screaming baby with a fever in the other room. Let me run, but let's do dinner tonight? I'll bring pizza." Amanda hung up without Samantha being able to respond, but she was glad that Amanda would be coming over. The company would be welcome.

"Pineapple pizza! Your favorite!" Amanda said as she pushed through the front door. Lunar leapt at her feet. "Hi Lunatic!"

"Lunar, go on out for a minute," Samantha said waving her hands at the door. Lunar took her orders and went onto the grass. "Cold enough out there?" Samantha asked Amanda as she took her coat off.

"Yup, winter's here. But, it's warming up because you have a date!"

"It's not really a date. We didn't call it that, but we left it open to be a date. So, it could be a date," Samantha stumbled over her words the way Lunar stumbled down the steps to go outside.

"Face it. It's a date. So, did he ask you or did you gather up the courage to ask him?"

"He asked me. We're going to the film festival. 'A Street Car Named Desire' is playing."

"Oh, that's not too depressing. Well, you make sure to have fun to balance it out. Is he picking you up?"

"No, we're meeting at the Thai House next to the theater."

"Hmm. Guess that's probably good for the first date, but it's not like you don't know him."

"It's just easier. That's the main reason. It's not like I live that close to town," Samantha justified.

Amanda helped herself to the plates and glasses while Samantha went to bring Lunar back in. When she came back in the kitchen, Amanda had set the table and placed slices of pizza on their plates. "So, how's the writing going anyway?" Amanda asked right before sticking a piece of crust in her mouth.

"I told you I finished my first one, right?" Amanda nodded and chewed. "Well, I started another one. I've written a handful of chapters already. I like it so far. It's a bit lighter than *Winter's Truth*, but not chick-lit either."

"Great, but what are you doing about getting *Winter's Truth* published? Did you send it to some publishers?" Amanda's question, Samantha knew, was more about financial worries.

"Actually, that's one thing that Craig has taught me. I need an agent."

"An agent? How does that work?"

"Just like an actor, I guess. I query agents and see if they're interested in my novel. If they are, I'll sign with them and then they sell it to the publishers. Makes sense when you think about it." Samantha reached into the pizza box and pulled another slice out, dragging mozzarella along the way.

"Have you sent this letter out? What is it? A query?"

Samantha couldn't keep the secret any longer. Between Amanda's underlying skeptical tone and the excitement of the Samantha's recent news, she had to tell her. "Well, actually, yes. I did send a handful of letters out and an agent asked to see the first three chapters?"

"What? When did this happen? That's terrific!"

"The letter came yesterday and I mailed the chapters out this morning." It felt good to release her secret and it lightened Amanda's concern.

"I wonder when she'll call you. Is that the next step?"

"I suppose. Call or e-mail. Unless she rejects it, then I'll get another self addressed envelope in the mail and that'll be it."

"No, don't think that. This will be good; I can feel it. Boy, this Craig guy is like a miracle in your life." Amanda dangled her pizza in midair and looked to the ceiling like she had just summonsed Samantha's angels in to help.

"Now don't go saying that! That's way too much pressure. He's a fellow writer who's been very helpful. That's it right now." Samantha wanted Amanda to be right, but a larger part of her was scared that she just might be right.

"Well, he seems to have helped you get over Robert, and that's a miracle considering where you were several months ago. Heck, even a month ago."

"He's certainly made a difference in my career. I've been fighting the rest of it off, and I must say, have done pretty good in that department." Samantha picked another slice of pizza out of the box. Lunar rested her head on Samantha's knee. "No, Lunar. No pizza for you." With that Lunar went back to her dog bed by the fireplace.

"That's the best way for a relationship to start. You'll see. I have a good feeling about this one. I knew all the others weren't right, and I haven't even met this guy, but I..."

"Okay, I get it. He sounds great. He is great. I can't deny that. I've just been ignoring it on some levels."

They finished their pizza and Amanda stood up from the table to gather her belongings. "Gotta go, early start tomorrow. Keep me posted though, kay?"

After Amanda left and Samantha cleaned up the kitchen, she decided to sit on the couch to write in her journal. She wasn't that tired, was still excited about the interested agent, and wasn't ready to climb into bed — a bad habit she had in the winter — getting in bed too early.

> *Today I sent the first three chapters of Winter's Truth to Ms. Jackson, the interested agent. I'm glad to have an agent who liked my query enough to ask for sample chapters. It kind of takes the pressure off a bit too. Now when I send out other queries, they won't go with such a sense of urgency.*

Her pen settled on the 'y' and a new idea came to her. She wondered what would happen if she drew pictures of the things she wanted in her journal? They would be safe from the public, so no one would witness her poor artistic abilities, but it would allow her to visualize her wishes in another way. Deciding

114

it was worth a try, she drew the front of a book store. That was easy, it's basically a box. Then the storefront window. Another box! And inside the window she drew a poster advertising her book signing for *Winter's Truth*. A rectangle!

The tricky part was drawing herself at the table actually signing the books. She attempted a face-on angle so that she wouldn't have to draw her profile. One step above a stick figure, she was now in black and white at a table signing copies of her book. She drew people lined up to the door, books in their hands, awaiting her signature. One of the men was tall dark and handsome — more in her mind than the rendition actually showed. Samantha put a thought bubble above his head and wrote, "I wonder if she'd go out with me?" inside of it. *There*, she thought. *My first book signing*. Her final touch was her car in the parking lot outside the book store. She'd wanted a Toyota Highlander for a while now, one of the new hybrid models, and so she drew a picture of one in the parking lot outside the book store. Satisfied with her drawing, she put the journal away and scooted down under the covers. Lunar had already settled in for the night.

Chapter VII

*T*he Thai restaurant was busy with people who had the same idea as Craig and Samantha, grabbing a bite to eat and a film festival movie. There were four theaters in town and this one had the most popular festival events. They managed to be seated in a fairly quiet section and their food came quickly. The movie started at seven, and it was only six o'clock now. Craig bought the tickets online the day before so they would be able to walk right in. Samantha liked the way he thought.

Wearing nice jeans, a v-neck cashmere sweater with a scarf, black boots and minimal jewelry, Samantha was a little more dressed up than what he had seen her in at the coffee shop. She paid extra attention to her makeup, especially the mascara. She felt put-together and confident. More so than on any previous first dates she'd had.

"What's the update on your novel?" she asked Craig when he wasn't chewing.

"I've finished the next round of drafts and put together six more query letters to send out on Monday. Just need to print the self addressed stamped envelopes."

"So even though you had an agent ask for sample chapters, you're still sending queries?"

Samantha was surprised that he wouldn't wait until he heard something from the first agent before bothering to send more queries.

"Have to for a few reasons. One, if they reject the work after reading the sample chapters, you want to be sure you have irons in the fire out there. Two, it keeps my mind off the agent who is reading the chapters. I can write about two to three thousand words a day, but that doesn't fill an entire day, so I send out more queries, enter contests. That kind of stuff."

"I see your point. I've been thinking about the agent I sent my chapters to more than I probably should. Every time the phone rings I jump and look at the caller ID to see if it's a New York area code. It's a lot of pressure, all this waiting."

"It can be if you let it get to you. Just keep focusing on your other book and go ahead and send out some more queries. Never know."

The theater was packed when they entered. "I'll get us some popcorn if you want to save some seats," Craig suggested. Samantha agreed and found her way through the double doors into the dark theater. Relieved, she found two seats by the isle and mid-way down. Couples filled most of the seats, some had their heads together whispering what Samantha assumed were loving notions. Some of the couples were young, some old, but most were about the same age as Craig and her. The nostalgia of the movie must have had a draw to thirty-something year-olds. Scanning the crowd, she surveyed each couple and tried to determine how long they'd been together or whether or not it was their first date. When she glanced down at the seats two rows in front of her, she felt her stomach surge to her throat. *Robert.* He sat there with his arms around a blond woman who couldn't have been older than thirty. The only light came from the screen. It showed the usual theater introduction—turn off your cell phone and spend lots of money on snacks while you're here. She didn't need much light though— she'd know his hair and his profile anywhere. Let alone the length and masculinity of his arm. The one wrapped around the blonde's shoulder. Scrunching down, Samantha slipped out from her seat, hoping to move back a few rows. When she stood up in the aisle and turned, she landed right in Craig's way, bumping the popcorn, which fell to her feet like snowflakes.

"Oh my God, I'm sorry," she said.

"No problem. There's still plenty. Where're you going?"

"Oh, those seats have popcorn on the floor and it's all sticky. Let's move back a bit." Samantha ushered him up a few rows and they took the only aisle seats remaining. Looking over her shoulder on the way, she made sure Robert hadn't heard her voice.

"Thanks for getting the popcorn," she said, leaning into Craig.

"Sure. There's a soda too. I just grabbed two straws. Hope you don't mind sharing. They're so big." Craig pointed a straw in her direction and Samantha took a sip before settling into her seat. The movie began, but her eyes were on Robert trying to evaluate the level of the relationship he was at with the blonde. This being the first time she'd seen him since they broke up, she wasn't sure how'd she'd handle the entire length of a movie with him just rows in front of her. Craig continued to unknowingly redirect her attention by offering her soda and popcorn.

Samantha sat motionless through much of the movie, as though Robert would be able to detect any movement as belonging to her. She managed just fine until Craig reached over and slipped his arm around her shoulder. The gesture made her feel smothered and trapped, but she didn't know how to undo it. His arm was there, and she didn't want to make a scene. Doing the best she could to endure the last half hour of the movie with the weight of Craig's arm around her neck, she was relieved when the credits began to roll.

The next challenge was exiting the theater before Robert saw her. She knew he would likely be nice and would want to make small talk. She didn't want small talk. Robert and the blonde stood up and worked their way through to the aisle. Craig released his arm from Samantha's shoulder just as she looked up and caught Robert's eye. The passionate kiss she turned and lay on Craig at that moment was a blend of fury and revenge. While he was receptive to her kiss, the people next to them and waiting to exit weren't.

"C'mon. Save it for later. We want to get out of here," screamed one lady.

"Right, sorry," Samantha said. Keeping her back to Robert, she gathered her purse and jacket. *Please God, let him have already passed by the time I turn around*, she thought. *It's only fair.*

"You okay?" Craig asked. He looked around the theater. "Let's get outside," he said.

"Sorry about that," Samantha said once they were in the clearing of the lobby. Craig took her hand and brought her out onto the street.

"You don't need to apologize for kissing me. I've wanted to kiss you for a long time," he said.

"What? You have?"

"Yes, can't you tell I'm crazy about you?"

As Craig spoke, Samantha looked over his shoulder at Robert and the blond walking hand and hand down the sidewalk, heads tucked together.

"Hello? Did you hear me?" Craig asked.

"Yes. Yes, I did. I'm just a little surprised by everything. It's all happening pretty fast, that's all."

Craig put his arm around her. They walked down the sidewalk in the opposite direction Robert had gone.

*****

Frothy soap blended between Samantha's palms and fingers. She lathered it over her face, washing away the remains of her previously applied makeup. She didn't normally wear this much makeup, but wanted to look as nice for Craig as she could. Her makeup was natural and no one could tell how much she was actually wearing until they saw her without it. Looking in the mirror, she thought about how she rarely washed her face before going to bed. She always washed it during her morning showers, but by nighttime she was either too tired or too lazy. On this night though, she made the extra effort to cleanse away the foundation, eye shadow, and whatever buildup had accumulated that evening.

Samantha's reflection in the mirror was pleasing to her—eyes bright, skin radiant, smile near perfect. *When did I become beautiful?* She wondered, and then splashed another handful of tepid water across her face, focusing on the nook between her nose and cheeks where the soap rested. Women only looked closely at their faces while applying or

121

removing their makeup, she determined. Fixing their hair didn't count since that focus was primarily on the peripheral of their face. She meant their actual face — skin, eyes, lips. *Maybe*, she thought, *I don't wash my face at night because it requires looking closely in the mirror.* The shower in the morning meant she didn't have to see a reflection, and while brushing her teeth, she often wandered into the bedroom and looked through her closet for what to wear, either to bed, or that day — always avoiding the mirror, subconsciously or consciously.

When Samantha raised her head from the sink and faced the mirror again, drops of water clung to her chin before landing in the porcelain bowl below, she remembered Craig's kiss. Her kiss to him. His return kiss. Their kiss on the sidewalk. It all overshadowed seeing Robert and the blonde. The antidote, she claimed, to forgetting a love was to fall in love again. But she had tried that for so many years and the perpetual ins and outs, ups and downs, always led her back to one place. Alone.

Chapter VIII

*W*e had a date," Samantha divulged to Ragnar the next Thursday. "We kissed, too."

"Wow, a date. Your first one since Robert. Also since you decided *not* to date. How'd it go?" Ragnar shifted in his seat.

"Actually, considering Robert was at the movie with his own date, it went quite well. I think I surprised myself, and I know I surprised Craig."

"Surprised him?"

"Yeah, well, Robert was heading toward us with his date, and I didn't want him to see me, so I instinctively turned and kissed Craig. Right there in the theater while everyone was trying to leave. That part wasn't fair, but once we were on the sidewalk, Craig and I talked a bit and kissed again. That time it was real and Robert didn't matter anymore."

"I'm not convinced it was Robert personally who set you on your downward spiral, if I can call it that, but rather that he just happened to be the one who made you shift gears."

Ragnar had hinted at this theory before, but until Samantha was ready to see it for herself; she dismissed the idea. Partly because she didn't want to believe that what she and Robert had wasn't real love. The essence of

123

him only being a temporary event couldn't compete with the love she thought they had.

"Could be. In hindsight all relationships are some form of a catalyst to another event. But true love, that's what stays. I know I sound like a hopeless romantic, but I have to believe that I will experience love in this lifetime. I just hope it's before I'm old and gray!" Samantha tugged at her hair, knowing the grays had already set in. But, she didn't feel old, so she still had time.

"I will say that the best thing about this is that you and Craig started out as friends before you let it turn romantic." Ragnar was writing on the legal pad as he verbalized his notion, as though taking credit for the success of it.

"Craig said that he's wanted to kiss me for a long time. That surprised me."

"You went out last Saturday, right? Have you been in contact or seen him since?"

"No, he's been out of town, but he returns tomorrow and we're going to do something. It's been kind of good to have space to reflect. That whole absence makes the heart grow fonder idea," Samantha said. "Now I just have to not blow this one."

"Don't look at it as being doomed before it's started," Ragnar said.

Samantha knew he was right, and considered the comment a slip. The Positive Journal was chock-full of positive attitudes and thoughts, but her dialogue with Ragnar fell back into its old routine, especially since she hadn't told him about the new journal. Maybe the habitual dialogue with Ragnar was contradictory to the concept of the journal? She could focus on speaking positively with Ragnar, but that almost defied the concept of therapy. Most of all, therapy in and of itself carried a negative connotation. She decided in that moment to take a break from Ragnar and see how she would do on her own again. Admittedly, she was happier than she could ever remember being and wondered if it was because of the new journal or Ragnar's sessions. In order to find out, she wanted to take a break from one or the other, and Ragnar was the one that made the most sense.

"You're right, and I usually do see a good outcome. Ya know, though, I've been thinking. Maybe I should take a break from our sessions. Kinda see how I do on my own. Does that make sense?" Samantha clutched her purse, waiting for his response. He didn't look shocked or disappointed, which pleased her.

"If you think so, that sounds fine. It's not like you don't know where to reach me. You've made tremendous progress, you know that?"

"Yes, I do. And I think that's why I need to let go of the crutch a bit. But, keep a space open for me around Christmas just in case I need ya!" Samantha said, hoping that wouldn't be the case. Ragnar smiled and nodded his now familiar nod. He made one final note on the legal pad, took a check from Samantha, and walked her to his door.

"You take care of yourself," was all that he said.

Samantha wondered if he usually knew when his patients weren't going to return, or did they simply stop calling and making appointments? The closure, even if it ended up being temporary, served as a launching point for her and gave her yet another sense of purpose.

By the next morning, Samantha realigned her focus on her novel. Fridays had become her easy day after several days in a row of pressing her fingers to the laptop keys. Although she wrote several more chapters that week, she had been distracted with thoughts of Craig and taking care of Lunar. Craig e-mailed her a few times a day and called every night. His traveling made him unreachable during that day, but he promised to call once back in town and so they could go out to dinner. Knowing he was returning that evening, Samantha wanted to put another chapter of her book behind her so that she could report her progress to him, not because she had to, but because she wanted to.

Amanda continued to live vicariously through Samantha, inhaling all of the romantic details of Samantha and Craig's date, their phone calls and e-mails, as though her own existence depended on it. Samantha was amused by this and at one point offered her former time slot with Ragnar to her best friend. "Really, it might help you too," she offered.

"Not on your life. No one needs to know how miserable my love life is, well lack of love life. I don't want anyone to tell me that I deserve all of the good things, blah blah blah."

"Your choice," Samantha said. In time she would tell her about the journaling, but didn't think that Amanda was the type to succumb to a ritual such as that, even if it meant leading her to happiness.

The coffee shop was still quiet at ten o'clock. The breakfast crowd had cleared out and the lunch crowd was still typing business letters, crunching numbers, enduring meetings, or making phone calls — not wanting to look at the clock yet because it wasn't anywhere near their company-imposed lunch time.

The tap on her shoulder as she concluded page one hundred and twenty three startled her. Her first guess was that Craig had returned early and knew he'd find her there, but when she turned around, she was face to face with Robert.

"Hey," was all he said.

"Hi." Samantha turned back to her laptop and resumed typing.

"C'mon Sam, don't do this. Talk to me." He took the liberty of sitting down at her table in the chair right beside her. When she didn't acknowledge him, he went a step further and placed his hand on her shoulder.

"Cut it out," she said in a hushed, angry voice. His hand fell to the wayside with the shrug of her shoulder. "I don't have anything to say to you."

"Will you just listen then? Please?" When his question went unanswered, he took the liberty of continuing, "I miss you. I really messed up."

"Right, okay. You've said what you came to say, now leave."

"Not until you tell me you'll come back to me."

Samantha coughed out her next words, "Go back to you? Are you crazy? Do you have any idea what you did to me? How I felt when you left?" By now she had turned and sat facing him.

"I do now. I miss being with you, talking to you," he said.

"What, blondes can't hold a conversation? Sorry to hear it, but I've moved on. I'm seeing someone, and I'm happier than I've been— probably in forever." Samantha looked him straight in the eye, hoping to deliver her point clearly, but it seemed to only challenge him.

"Who, that guy at the theater? He's not for you. I could tell."

128

"No, you don't think so? Well, he's done more for me in one date than you did in the entire few months that we dated. And it's not just about him. I'm happy with my life now. I'm writing, I have a puppy…"

"You got a dog?"

"Yeah, Amanda gave it to me for my birthday. But that's beside the point. I'm writing my second novel, I go to bed without crying." Samantha stopped herself. "Why am I even telling you this? I have nothing to say to you." She shoved her chair away from the one he had taken over, pulling her laptop with her. Somewhat disappointed in her over-reaction, she still made her point.

"But, you still miss me, right?"

"You're not getting it. You and all of the others represented the old Samantha. The new one wants nothing to do with you or anyone else who hurt me." Robert looked at her, started to say something, but stopped himself. "Glad to see you're getting it now. So leave."

"Can't."

"Do it, Robert."

"I've never fought for anyone before," he said. "I want to fight for you."

Samantha laughed, "Oh, that's a good one. Save it for blondie or whomever else you've dated since you left me. They might just believe that line."

Robert stood up from his chair and took a step toward the door. "I'm not giving up, Sam.

129

When this guy dumps you, it's me you'll call. I'll be waiting." He turned and left the shop, taking one last look at her through the window. The only reason Samantha noticed him looking was because her seat faced the window. He waved and she ignored him. But, the encounter distracted her enough from being able to go back to work on her novel. She packed up her laptop and drove home.

"Lunar, let's go for a walk," she called when she entered the front door. Breaking the speed limit to get home didn't release enough of her tension. A walk would do the trick though. Lunar scampered across the floor, wagging her tail in excitement, and waited for Samantha to pet her. When her affection was met, Lunar pushed through to the door in anticipation of the promised walk.

"Okay, okay. Let's go," Samantha said.

Once outside, although the air was chilled, Samantha immediately started to feel better. The brisk walk down her road passed by a few other cottages and select farms. The walk, met with the fresh air, was the perfect combination for releasing Robert's negative energy off of her. Telling him to leave was a combination of making sure she wouldn't break down and want him back, but also that she really didn't want him back. She had moved on with her life and he had hurt her too much for her to trust him again. Craig was so much more than Robert could ever be, and she appreciated that more each day. If it weren't for Craig, she wouldn't have learned about agents and the publishing industry in general, but it was more than that. There was something beneath the surface of it all. He liked her for her. Day after day over the past month he engaged her in conversations at the coffee shop and was always respectful of her keeping him at arm's length — until their first official date. Letting her guard down that night, trusting him with her kiss, shifted her thinking. This time though, she had an ammunition that she hadn't had with past relationships, she had her happiness and her confidence.

Samantha hadn't noticed that her walk churned itself into more of a jog as they progressed down the road. Lunar ran along side, stopping only on occasion to sniff. The approaching corner told Samantha that she had gone over two miles. The digital display on her watch indicated that it was three forty-eight. "Lunar, we need to get back to the house! Craig should be calling anytime now," she said. Lunar looked up at her. "Yes, Craig's coming home. You haven't met Craig yet, but I think you'll like him."

Samantha jogged her way back down the side of the road to the cabin. Only one car passed them, her elderly neighbor Mr. Johansson. He often offered to do work around her yard, but she never felt right letting him. She didn't want to be responsible if he were

131

injured. Sometimes when she had been in a deep depression and did nothing but bake cookies, she'd bring him a batch. He was always appreciative.

At the entry of the driveway, she stopped and pulled her mail from the mailbox. Mixed in with her usual mail were two new self addressed stamped envelopes.

"Two more, Lunar!"

Once inside, she tossed the other mail aside and opened the two that held critical information about her novel. She began to read the first one, "Dear Author, Thank you for your query. Although we are sure your work holds merit, we don't feel we're the right agency to represent you..." she didn't bother reading the next paragraph.

"That's okay 'cause I've got Ms. Jackson reading my chapters. That agent doesn't know what they're missing, huh Lunar?"

Samantha opened the next letter, which began with "Dear Author," but the next sentence was different. "We were intrigued by your query and would be interested in viewing the first three chapters of your novel."

"Oh my God! It's another hit!" Samantha jumped up and down waving the letter in the air until she was dizzy. She landed on the couch and Lunar jumped up and licked her face, joining in on the excitement. Samantha read the letter two more times to make sure it said what she thought it had said. It was true, they wanted her sample chapters.

The phone rang, breaking into her third read of the letter.

"Hello?" she said without looking at the caller ID.

"Hey! You sound like you're in a good mood."

"Robert, I told you not to contact me."

"Well, it's Friday night and I thought I could convince you to go out. C'mon Sam."

"Did you not hear what I said to you at the coffee shop today? No. Never. Now stop calling." She hung up, angry that he had interfered with her moment of delight.

The phone rang again. "I said, no!"

"Oh, well okay. I guess we're not going out tonight?"

"Oh, my God! Craig! I'm sorry. I thought you were someone else," Samantha's voice softened. "Lots of solicitors calling this afternoon."

"Want me to call back? We can start over?"

"No, it's okay. I just wish you had called a few minutes ago when I was elated. Guess what?"

"Um, you finished your second novel?"
"Now that would be ambitious. Guess again."

"You heard from another agent."

"And…"

"And they said that you're query made them sit up and take notice and they want to read more."

"Yes, how'd you know?" Samantha twirled her hair with her fingers.

"Just a hunch. What else would make you so elated? Isn't that what you were? Elated?"

"Well, admittedly, not much else. But, dinner with you would rate high up on the list. Are you home?" Samantha found herself anxious to see him.

"Yup. Just got in. I'm kind of in the mood for casual since I've been on the road all day. Why don't I bring something over? If that's okay."

"Sure, that sounds fine. You choose." Samantha was relieved to not have to go back out again. She gave him directions to her cabin and when they hung up, she turned on the porch light.

Returning to the living room, she looked around and panicked.

"Damn! This place is a mess!" She tossed the magazines into a wicker basket that sat on the floor at the end of the couch, put the last bit of dishes in the dishwasher and wiped down the countertops. She ran a rag across the sink in the downstairs bathroom before running upstairs to change. After deciding on a different pair of jeans and a pink turtleneck sweater, she ventured to the bathroom to reapply her makeup. Within an hour she had

134

the house tidied, herself put together, and made a quick call to Amanda to tell her about the agent and that Craig was coming over for dinner.

"Damn, girl. You're on a roll. Men, agents. What's next?"

"I dunno. A contract with an agent would be the next best thing to happen. I've gotta run, I hear his car in the driveway. I'll call you tomorrow." Samantha hung up on Amanda without waiting for a response.

When the doorbell rang a few seconds later, Samantha took one last look in the reflection of the hallway mirror. Lunar pounced on Craig's feet when the door opened.

"Well, hello there little pup. Aren't you cute?" Craig bent down and scratched Lunar on the head. She obviously agreed with him that she was cute and was bound to show him just how cute she was. "This must be Lunar?" Craig smiled and bent down to pet Lunar.

"Yup, that's my lunatic pup, Lunar." Samantha said.

When Craig stood up, he leaned over and kissed Samantha. First a hello kiss, and after she welcomed that, a full kiss.

"Mmmm. It's good to see you," he said.

"You too. I missed having you around," Samantha admitted. "C'mon in the kitchen and unload your armful." Samantha led the way down the hall to her kitchen.

"Nice little cottage you have here," he said from behind her, Lunar at his feet.

"It's perfect for me. Just the right size and it's quiet out here but still close enough to town. Did you have any problems finding it?"

Samantha helped him unload the large paper bag he put down on the counter. Grilled chicken, pasta salad, and a mix of vegetables. There was a smaller bag within the bag that Craig pulled out.

"Dessert," he said. "You have to wait until after dinner though."

Samantha set out plates, silverware and napkins. "I've got sodas, water, juice, and wine. What's your choice?"

"Red wine?"

"Yup. It's in the cabinet over there," Samantha said pointing to one over his shoulder. He turned around and retrieved a bottle after looking at the options.

"This one okay?"

"Any of them is fine with me."

"Great. Hey, before we sit down to eat, let me see the letter."

Samantha had been so excited to see him, she nearly forgot about the letter. "It's in my office, this way." Craig followed her down the hall into her office. She handed him the envelope and he took the liberty of removing the letter and reading it. A smile formed across his face.

"So, that's cool, huh?" she said.

"It's way cool. Congratulations." He put the letter back in the envelope and handed it back to her. When she reached out, he took her by the hand, pulled her in and kissed her. This time the kiss was longer and more passionate than the one in the hallway. She curled into his arms, letting the letter fall to the desk. In his next breath, he said, "That agent would be crazy not to take you on."

Over dinner they talked about his trip. He went to a writing conference in New York City that he had signed up for a while ago. Samantha decided she would go the next year. He told her about the agents he met and the other writers who participated. After dinner he helped her with the dishes and they settled in on the couch.

"Read me some of your book," he said.

"What? As I recall, you've already read some of it," Samantha poked him gently in the ribs.

"Well, just a few pages. C'mon read some of it to me. I know you have a print of it somewhere around here." He lifted a few pillows from the couch, pretending to look for her manuscript.

"Very funny. Okay. I'll read you a few pages of the first chapter, but that's it." Samantha went to her office and retrieved the printed manuscript.

"Remember, it's a chick book," she said when she came back down the hall. Craig was lying on the couch when she returned. She took a seat and he pulled her down next to him. Lying side by side, she read the first, then the second page of the chapter. By the third page, he was kissing her neck. The forth and remaining pages of the chapter floated to the ground next to the couch. Embraced, legs intertwined, and lips alternating on one another's neck and then back to the other's lips, they acted like teenagers home alone making out on the couch.

Though she was over five-foot-eight and had legs longer than most women, his legs were still able to wrap completely around hers, tucking her in closer to him. Pressed against his chest, she felt warm and safe in a way she hadn't experienced before. His left arm reached around her back and up to her ear, which he swirled with his fingertip. Her fingers slipped through his dark curls, sliding until she reached the end of them then returning to his scalp to start over again. The combination of kissing him and running through the locks of soft curls pacified Samantha and if that was all they did that night, she would have been content. Craig, apparently, felt the same way. He continued stroking her neck and ear, continued to kiss her, but never pushed it further than that. Amazed at his tenderness, Samantha felt herself falling deeper into his chest.

"Are you comfortable?" Craig asked her.

"Yes. How could I not be?" She smiled up at him, looking at the crest of his cheekbones, the dimple in the center of his chin, and where his lips met his cheeks.

He touched her chin in return, turning it up toward him. "I missed you," he said then cupped her chin and pulled it till her mouth met his.

Four hours later he stood at her doorway and said goodnight. "Thank you for an incredible evening."

"Thanks for bringing dinner."

"Anytime if that's the thanks I get. You make me feel good." He laughed at her and pulled her in for one last hug.

"You make me feel good, too," she said. "Geez, as a couple of writers, you'd think we could be more original."

"Sometimes the words don't do the describing," he said. "Good night. I'll call you in the morning."

She watched as he walked to his car. Lunar ran out into the yard for her last romp before bed.

"Good night," she called as he opened the car door and lowered himself into the front seat.

Upstairs she wrote in her journal, "I deserve to be happy. It's that simple."

She added a few more notes about the agent's request, because that too was a very positive event to write about that day. She couldn't remember being this happy and was suddenly afraid of losing it all.

"I'm not going to lose everything this time. I deserve all of this," she said to herself. With that thought, she fell asleep.

Chapter IX

*B*y the middle of November Samantha had sent out over twenty query letters and four agents had requested sample chapters. Craig assured her that the ratio was impressive, although she wasn't sure if he was saying so just to be nice. In her research online, she realized that she was somewhere in the middle of what most authors were experiencing and decided that was good enough. Her decision was based on the intent of keeping her thoughts positive.

Thanksgiving was approaching and Samantha was starting to make plans. In the past, she and Amanda went out to dinner together, especially when they were both single. This year Samantha decided to invite Amanda over so she could meet Craig. He hadn't mentioned going away or having dinner with anyone else. His family consisted of his parents and a brother, but they all lived in Arizona. When she met him at the coffee shop the Thursday before, she broached the subject with him.

"So, I'm thinking of inviting Amanda over for Thanksgiving. What are your plans?"

"I hadn't thought about it, really. Other than hoping to spend it with you." Craig gave her his best puppy dog eyes.

141

"That's what I was hoping. I thought it would be great for you to meet Amanda and we can cook up a turkey and the fixin's. How does that sound?"

Craig reached across the table and kissed her.

"Perfect," he said.

They now shared a table at the coffee shop and she no longer huddled in the corner. They made a rule that they had to let each other write for one hour increments without disruption unless the shop was on fire or their e-mail popped up with an agent responding positively. Other than that, peace and quiet. At the end of the hour, they gave each other an update on word count and character development for a few minutes before delving back in.

By lunchtime they had both written their fair share of pages. Craig went up to the counter and ordered Samantha her favorite sandwich and something for himself. While he was at the counter ordering, she went online to check her e-mail, which displayed 10 new messages. The habit of skimming her e-mails in search of the subject line "re: your query" had long been formed. But, this time in the sixth e-mail down, the subject line read, "Please send more."

When Samantha opened the full e-mail, she continued to read, "Dear Ms. Sounder, We were very impressed by your query and would like for you to send us the entire manuscript for review. While we normally ask for sample chapters, your project is one that jumped out and we would like to expedite the process. Please send the manuscript and a bio to our address listed below. Kind regards, Sylvia Somers."

"Oh my god! Craig! Come here!" Samantha shouted across the coffee shop, which was now filled with lunch crowd chatter so the decibel she reached went ignored for the most part.

"What's wrong?" Craig came back to the table with two plates in hand. "I need to go back for our drinks," he said.

"They can wait. Come read this," Samantha said as she pulled her chair to the side so he could settle in close to the laptop. He placed the plates on the table and leaned into the screen to read it. His eyes widened and he reached over and put his hand on her back while he read the rest. "Wow! That's very promising Ms. Sounder," he emphasized her last name.

"The full manuscript!" Samantha sat back in her chair and read the e-mail one more time while Craig went to grab their drinks from the counter. "I need to stop and pick up some paper on my way home," she told him as he returned.

"Ink too," he said.

That afternoon Samantha entered her cottage with paper and ink and sat down to write a cover letter while the printer churned out her manuscript, which was nearly three hundred pages. She paid close attention, making sure her contact information was correct: street address, phone number, e-mail. It was all there, all correct. The header on the remaining pages stated her name, the manuscript's name, and the page number all in the top left corner. The letter she had sent to the other agent worked as a template. All she had to change was "sample chapters" to "full manuscript" as well as the agent name and address. She included a note in the introductory paragraph that she was equally excited about their response to her query. She didn't want to over do it, be too flowery. Just professional and positive, and when the letter printed out on top of the last page of the manuscript, she read it once more and was satisfied with its wording. She signed it, packed everything together and put it on the kitchen counter to mail.

"There's still another hour before the post office closes. Should we go, Lunar?"

Lunar, always ready when she heard the word "go," ran to the door where her leash was. She already understood the difference between "out" and "go." There was no leash required when she was just going "out," whereas "go" meant a ride in the car, and hence the leash.

The sun was dropping below the ridge of the mountains and by time Samantha reached the post office at five minutes before five, she had to turn on her headlights. There were two people in line when she walked in, and they only purchased stamps.

When it was her turn, Samantha handed the package to the clerk and said, "First class, please."

She watched the clerk set her package on the scale, then she paid the postage and watched some more as it landed in a bin with a pile of other packages, just like the one she sent out a few weeks ago had. Certain that the manuscript was on its way to New York City, Samantha climbed back into her car where Lunar awaited her in the back seat. Just as she turned the key to start her car, her cell phone rang.

"Hello?" she said.

"Hey, Ms. Sounder. It's me. What're you up to?" Craig's voice on the other end of the phone was exactly what she wanted to hear.

"Just left the post office where I mailed off not just sample chapters, but my entire manuscript. God, it felt so good!"

"I'm sure it felt great. Are you heading home?"

"That was the plan."

"Can I meet you there? I'm out your way as it is," Craig asked.

"Yeah, I'll be there in twenty." Samantha hung up glad that she was going to get to see him again that day. When they left the coffee shop earlier she was so focused on going home to print her manuscript that they hadn't talked about plans for later.

The trees that lined her driveway were now a bare form of themselves. It was dark and she had forgotten to turn on her porch light in the excitement of going to the post office. Craig's car wasn't there yet, so she left her headlights on so she could see while she went inside and turned on the porch light. As she walked back outside to shut off the headlights and to lock the car, she spotted Craig's headlights illuminating the road. Lunar was off in the yard somewhere, probably happy to be out of the car again.

"There's my girl," Craig said as he walked toward her. Samantha stood and watched as he reached into the back seat and when he emerged, his face was blocked by the largest bouquet of flowers she had ever seen, let alone received.

"What are those?" she said, gleefully.

"For you," he leaned over from behind the flowers and planted a kiss on her lips. "Let's go inside, it's cold out here."

Samantha was slightly suspicious of his behavior, but obliged him by going inside. Her curiosity peaked, she closed the door, took the flowers from him and headed toward the kitchen.

"So, what did I do to deserve this visit?"

"Actually, it's a combination celebration," Craig smiled slyly at her, clearly busting to tell her something.

"Well, tell me!" Samantha said as she took a vase from the cabinet and filled it with water.

"Need you to sit down."

"Okay, go have a seat on the couch. I'll be right there."

Craig sat down on the couch where Lunar lay at his feet. She was instantly fond of him and had no problems letting him know.

"Now," Samantha said as she sat down next to him. "What is this about?"

Craig took her hands and clutched them in his.

"I got an agent!" he spat out.

"What? Ohmygod! Who, which one?"

Samantha tightened her grip on his hands and before he could finish his answer, she leaned into him and kissed him. Releasing his hands from hers, he wrapped them around her back and neck.

"It's the one in New York that asked for a full right before I met you. Roger Lee Peters. He called this afternoon. I can't believe it. I'm going into the city next week to meet with him. He offered to Fed-Ex the contract, but I wanted to meet him in person. I think that's better. Don't you?"

147

"Yeah. Yes, definitely. This is so awesome!"

"I know you'll get picked up soon too. You have to," Craig said.

The next kiss was less congratulatory and more passionate. They fell into each other's arms on her couch, melting together. His hands stroked her back and found themselves on her hips. She reached around and put a hand in his pocket, gently squeezing him. The kissing intensified. Taking his hand, she stood and led him toward the stairs. Her passion building with each climb of the steps; he trailed her, gripping her hand. They landed on her bed, entangled in arms and legs; he somehow managed to pull her sweater up over her head, revealing her flat stomach and the curves of her breasts. She tugged the bottom of his sweater out from his jeans, and then pulled it up and over his head. Unbuttoning his shirt, one at a time revealed the crests of each muscle and the tuff of hair in the middle of his chest. She ran her fingers through the hair while he unbuttoned her jeans, then pulled apart the sides so that the zipper would unzip, exposing her satin pink panties to him. Kissing his shoulders, she pressed his shirt back over them and down his arms until it tumbled to the bed, landing gently on her pillow. His hands reached into her pants, tugging them down to her knees, she lifted each leg allowing him to completely remove them. Lying there in her pink panties and blue lace bra, she mouthed, "I want you," and yanked his jeans off. They lay together, the light casting a shadow on the wall of two becoming one. Caressing, kissing, grasping, breathing.

Craig looked up at the ceiling when they finished, Samantha curled into his chest. Neither spoke, only stroked hair, arms, hips. Samantha let out a shiver; Craig pulled the comforter over them and they fell asleep.

11:17 p.m. was what the clock read when Samantha rolled over and looked at it. It was shortly after that when she remembered that Craig was in her bed curled up beside her. The warmth of his body should have been the immediate give away, but it was the memory of making love with him that cultivated the feelings stirring inside of her. Careful not to wake him, she eased her way out from under the covers, knowing that Lunar wouldn't make it until morning without having to go out. Lying on the floor at the foot of the bed, Lunar thumped her tail on the carpet in agreement.

Finding her robe in the dark closet was a challenge for Samantha, especially without making a sound. The door squeaked when she closed it—she immediately looked at Craig, hoping to not stir him. His head lay on her pillow, shadowed by the cast of moonlight through the window. She hadn't shut the blinds. It was only six-thirty when they collapsed onto her bed in the memorable throws of passion. Tip-toeing down the stairs, she was finally able to turn on a light in the downstairs hallway. Thankful that Lunar was quick with her outing, they tiptoed back upstairs and Samantha climbed back under the covers.

"You're cold," Craig mumbled into her ear.

"Oh, I'm sorry. I didn't want to wake you, let alone freeze you."

Craig pulled her into him, "Actually it feels good. It was hot under these covers." He ran his fingers down her waist to her hips and pulled her in even closer to him. "What time is it?"

"Around eleven thirty."

"Mmmm."

"Go back to sleep, hun," she said.

The sun shined into Samantha's eyes and woke her at six thirty. That was the one thing about day light savings, mornings were brighter, which balanced the dark evenings, but only if you were awake early enough to enjoy them. They woke up together, took a shower together, and she made them French toast for breakfast before they left and headed to the coffee shop.

Later that afternoon when Samantha was home alone, she pulled out her Positive Journal and wrote,

> *Craig stayed over last night after we made love. Wow. Simply wow. His body is so warm and welcoming. I've never been this*

happy. Meanwhile, my new novel is flowing so readily, as though it's been written in my head for several years or lifetimes and all I had to do was put pen to paper. I'm loving the characters, the plot flow...all of it.

She clasped the journal closed and stashed it in her nightstand drawer, its new home unexposed to visitors.

Chapter X

*C*raig went to New York that Monday and met with his agent. Samantha stayed home to work on her novel, and when he returned on Tuesday night, he went straight over to her house where they celebrated with dinner, wine, and making love. With all the excitement of Craig finding an agent and Samantha sending in a full manuscript, Thanksgiving seemed to just blend in to it all. But, the actual holiday would also stop their work lives for a day; No mail arrived for Samantha from agents, No phone calls from New York. Samantha's cottage was filled with food, Lunar, Craig and Amanda. They cooked a turkey, potatoes, and veggies. Amanda brought both pumpkin and apple pie. Craig brought vanilla ice cream to top them with — everyone's personal favorite.

Amanda and Craig hit it off, as Samantha knew they would. Their common topic was Samantha, but much to Samantha's relief, they found other interesting things to discuss.

"Sammy, remember the time we drove to DC just to see all of the museums, then turned around and drove home?" Amanda called to the kitchen after dinner. Samantha was doing the dishes while Craig and Amanda sat on the couch drinking wine and sharing stories.

"Yes, I remember. You wouldn't let me drive your car because I stepped in some kid's gum and couldn't get it off the bottom of my shoe. You were sure it would stick to the pedal and we'd get in an accident somehow. That never made sense to me." Samantha rinsed the last dish and put it in the dishwasher while she listened to Amanda tell the rest of the story.

"She was certain the museum's security guard was following us like we were going to steal a stegosaurus." Amanda and Craig both laughed and when Samantha walked into the living room, he pulled her onto his lap. "Oh Sammy, it's so good to see you so happy. You deserve it," Amanda said.

"Yeah, I am happy," Samantha said. Craig pulled Samantha to him and kissed her.

"Okay, that's my cue to leave," Amanda said and stood up.

"No, you don't have to," Samantha insisted.

"I should though. I want to get home before the turkey's sleeping drug kicks in. That or I'll be passed out on your ouch."

"Are you sure you're okay to drive?" Craig asked. "You had a few glasses of wine, ya know."

"Yes, I'm fine." Amanda walked over and grabbed her coat from the rack by the door.

"Here I fixed a to-go package for you. I can't eat all of the leftovers," Samantha said, handing over three Tupperware's full of goodies in a plastic bag. "Thanks for bringing the pies too!" Samantha walked Amanda to the door and turned on the porch light for her. It wasn't until the taillights were out of view that she closed the door and went back to the living room. Craig was lying on the couch, eyes closed. She went over and lay on top of him.

"Uggggh," he moaned from underneath her. "Feels like you had your share of dinner," he teased.

"Funny."

"Amanda's great. I'm glad you have such a good friend," Craig said.

"She's gotten me through a lot. I just wish she were more open to falling in love again. She has so much going for her: Her own pediatrician practice, a house, good looks, and funny. What man wouldn't want that?"

"I dunno. But, I do know who I want."

They made love on the couch and went upstairs to bed where they made love again.

"Can you get used to this?" Samantha asked.

"To what?"

"Making love as much as we do."

"Gee, let me think about it. Yes," he said immediately. "If it's with you, yes."

"You wouldn't get tired of it?"

"No. Never."

Samantha believed him. She had an unusually active sexual appetite, but it wasn't only her sex drive. It was the way Craig made

154

her feel in his arms — safe and warm — the way every woman would want.

"Do you know how good you make me feel?" she asked him in between love making sessions.

"If it's close to how you make me feel, then yes, I do know. But don't ask me to describe it because even as a writer, I don't know that I could put it into words."

Craig wrapped his legs around Samantha and they lay there in silence. She couldn't find the words either, and left it at his last comment before they fell asleep.

The next Monday Samantha left the coffee shop early. She had to take Lunar to the vet for her shots and didn't want to be late for her first vet appointment. Craig was working on a few edits that the agent suggested for his first book and stayed behind. When she said goodbye to him, they agreed to meet up later that evening.

When Samantha pulled down the driveway, she could see Lunar's face through the living room's bay window.

"Be right there!" Samantha called to her as she went to the mailbox. When she opened the box, there were just two letters. Her stomach sank; she didn't want to read any bad news, although she wasn't sure why she thought either might be. There was no reason to be, except for another rejection from another agent. She was used to those. She opened the first letter, and discovered that what her gut felt was true... it was a rejection from Ms. Jackson. She indicated that while Samantha had an enjoyable writing style, she didn't think she was the right agent to represent her and wished her luck with finding one that would. While the tone was encouraging, the message was clear — one big agent down.

The second letter was another self addressed stamped envelope. Samantha opened it, which didn't take much doing since it hadn't been sealed, and there inside was air. *Nothing. Zip. Nada.* Her first reaction was one of frustration. The envelope itself had a crease in it, clearly where it was slightly crunched by one of the postal machines. And since it was a self addressed the return address was none other than her own. The meter stamp indicated that it had been mailed from zip code 100--, surely a New York City agent.

Samantha checked her spreadsheet of agents and narrowed it down to three possible agents. She supposed that as the others responded, she'd be able to narrow it down further. For a moment she felt as though this was a plot in a movie or another author's book where someone sends a letter with life changing information and the letter gets lost in post office frenzy, leaving fate to step in and help it find its way to the recipient. Maybe fate would step in or maybe she'd simply be able to narrow it down as the others responded. Either way, there was nothing more she could do about the empty envelope except to add it to the pile of rejections on her desk.

The drive to the vet's office felt laborious. She didn't want to have to be cheery with anyone. While they sat in the waiting room, Samantha forced herself to change her thoughts to positive ones. She continued to write in her journal everyday, but some days she didn't write because Craig was there and she needed privacy. On the days she knew he'd be there, she wrote in the mornings or afternoons. Her journal writing continued to propel her thoughts into staying optimistic, but until now she had no reason to not be positive. Being rejected by Ms. Jackson was Samantha's first real test to stay on a positive track, and when she recognized the test on a conscious level, she was able to see it in another light. She decided then and there that Ms. Jackson was right...she wasn't the best agent for Samantha and there was a better fit out there.

"Lunar, the vet is ready for you," called the receptionist.

"Let's go, Lunar," Samantha said. She stood up and led the pup into the exam room where she hoisted Lunar up onto the exam table and gave her a treat out of glass jar on the counter. They had been working on "sit" and "stay". Lunar did both and wolfed down the treats. "Guess you're not too worried about receiving shots, huh?"

The veterinarian walked in the door. His square jaw line, defined lips, and captivating hazel eyes took Samantha by surprise. She half expected an old-timer, but wasn't sure why. Her neighbor had recommended this vet after using him for several years. He couldn't have been much more than fifty, but was more likely in his mid-forties.

"Good afternoon, I'm doctor Whitmore," he said. "This must be Lunar?"

"Yes, and I'm Samantha," Samantha said, suddenly wishing she had run a brush through her hair while still in the parking lot.

He nodded at Samantha, opened Lunar's file, and reiterated the little bit of data that was in it.

"So, she's here for her shots and exam. Okay, let's take a look." He placed the chart on the counter behind him and stepped toward the exam table. "You are cute, aren't you?"

"Thanks, I think she is too."

"How long have you had her?"

"A few months. She was a birthday present from a friend." Samantha leaned against the table and scratched Lunar behind the head, giving her treats while Dr. Whitmore examined her.

"Nice gift," he said, glancing up at Samantha.

The hazel in his eyes reflected the light above him. She glanced down at his hands, admiring their strength and smoothness. *What am I doing? Stop it*, she reminded herself. Craig has everything you want.

"Is she your first puppy or dog?"

"Yes. My sister's allergic, so we never had any growing up. Guess you could say Lunar and I are learning together. But, I dated a guy who had a German Shepherd. A very large German Shepherd who slept in his bed. Lunar sleeps at my feet or on the floor, but she's not over one hundred pounds with thick wiry hair," Samantha rambled. "Besides, she still has puppy breath," she added.

"So, I'm guessing that relationship didn't work out?" Dr. Whitmore reached into a drawer and pulled out a syringe. At the sight of it, Samantha sat down. "Don't like needles?" he asked.

"No. I faint when I get shots. I thought I could handle her getting one though." Samantha turned away and faced the wall. Embarrassed, Samantha tried to cover her weakness with conversation. "So, how long have you been a vet?" *Too obvious.*

"Ten years now. Can't imagine doing anything else. You?"

"I'm a writer. Nor can I imagine doing anything else." Samantha peaked to see if he was done and when she saw him putting the needle in the red box marked "Hazard

Materials Only" with the crossbones on it, she resumed her position next to Lunar and made it up to her by providing kisses to the top of her fuzzy head.

"A writer, eh? Anything I know?" this time he stopped what he was doing and looked right at her.

"Not yet. I've finished my first novel and am working on my second. Trying to find an agent too." Samantha gave Lunar another treat.

"Well, if you want I can check with my sister. She's an agent in New York City." Dr. Whitmore said this like it was as simple as picking up the telephone.

"What? She is? Do you know what genre she represents?" Samantha wasn't willing to give herself permission to have it so easy yet.

"I think literary, some commercial and some women's. I can ask her for you. I might even have her card in the back if you want to query her." *Wow, he knows what a query is.* Not surprising, but the conversation was not one she'd expect to be having with a veterinarian. "Let me go look for it. Lunar can get down if she wants—everything looks great and she handled the shot like a champ." He left the room through the same door that he had entered through. Samantha was now even more embarrassed that she was afraid of needles. Hopefully he wouldn't tell his sister that.

He returned to the room a few minutes later with a business card in hand.

"Go ahead and send her your manuscript. No need to query. I'll be talking to her and will give her the heads up." Dr. Whitmore handed her the card with a wink. "Good luck. I hope it works out for you."

"Gosh, thanks! This is really terrific. I've had a couple of agents show interest, so I know I'm on the right path. But, every connection helps. I really appreciate this."

Samantha took Lunar by her leash, put the card in her purse, thanked him once more and paid the bill with the receptionist. That was when it really hit her. With Lunar in the backseat, head out the window, they headed home to print her manuscript one more time.

While still in the car, she called Craig, who answered on the third ring.

"Hey, hun! How'd the vet go?" he asked.

"Better than expected. Other than my fear of needles, we did great. She did great. Guess what though?" Samantha was beaming ear to ear.

"Um, you got a lollipop and she got a biscuit?" he joked.

"No, bigger than that."

"Oh. You got a stuffed animal and she got a biscuit."

"Cute. No. Better, not bigger."

"I give up, but I can tell you're psyched about whatever it is."

"Dr. Whitmore's sister is an agent! He gave me her card. Said I can send the entire script and that he would give her heads up that it's on the way. Isn't that awesome? What're the odds?"

"Geez, that's a great connection. Make sure to mention him in the cover letter, but I know you know that. Maybe this'll be the one!" Craig said then coughed into the phone.

"Are you getting sick?" Samantha asked.

"Little bit. I should stay home tonight and let you get your work done. How 'bout we meet at the shop in the morning. I'll be there by eight thirty."

"Sounds good. Feel better. Do you have soup or something?" Samantha was relieved to have a night to herself to catch up on work around the house and to prepare the package. If Craig were there with her, she would be too distracted.

It wasn't until she walked through her door and looked around the cottage that she realized how much needed to be done. She'd been so busy with Thanksgiving Day, having Craig around, and mailings to agents that her cottage took on a familiar look from months ago. When she first got Lunar, she had the place in tip-top, puppy-proof shape and for weeks enjoyed the cleanliness. Her goal that night was to bring the cottage back to that state and to prepare her manuscript to send to Dr. Whitmore's sister. She took the business card out of her purse and read her name, Katie Gary. "Okay Ms. Gary, we'll see what you say."

By seven-thirty, the kitchen sink was so clean she could make a sandwich in it, the living room was dust-free, the carpets were vacuumed, and the ceramic tiles sparkled. Anything that made her cringe when she looked at it was cleaned, filed or put away. Every tracked in leaf, every stain or spot of food on the countertops, and every paper was dealt with.

The release of energy from cleaning and the sight of the final result left her feeling much better about life, her cottage, and especially her earlier rejection. She was ready to sit down at the computer and write her cover letter while the manuscript printed once again. The final touch...labels...were made at eight-thirty and by nine o'clock, she collapsed into bed. Almost too tired to write in her Positive Journal, she mustered the energy since she had so much to say.

> *Turns out Dr. Whitmore's sister is an agent. He gave me her card and said to send her the full manuscript. Wouldn't that be great if she took me on as a client? Maybe the connection will help, but I want her to take me on because of the*

merit of my work, as I'm sure she would only do. I'm glad to have the chance to work with her.

Poor Craig is sick, so he stayed home tonight. I was able to really clean this place up again. It always feels so much better when it's clean and tidy. I didn't think I'd ever be the type of person to become obsessive about keeping a clean house, but I can see how once you go down that road it's hard to turn back. I'm thinking about reading some books on Feng Shui. Lunar had a great checkup with the vet too…

The phone rang, interrupting her writing.

"Hello?"

"Hey, it's me! I wanted to say goodnight," Craig said.

"Hi. How're you feeling?"

"A bit better. I slept for an hour, woke up and thought about you. Then I had some dinner, but I'm about to go back to bed, so I thought I'd call to say goodnight." Craig coughed a few times into the phone. "Sorry 'bout that."

"Oh don't worry. I'm glad you called and that you slept," Samantha said. "You didn't miss much here. I cleaned the house and printed the script out."

"Oh, but I did. I missed you."

"Me too. You get some sleep, and I'll see you in the morning," Samantha said.

They hung up and Samantha finished her entry about Lunar before adding,

> *Craig called to say goodnight. What a sweetie.*

Samantha leaned over, tucked the journal back into the drawer, and turned out the light. Lunar curled up against her feet. "Goodnight, Lunar," Samantha said. She slept through the night without any nightmares.

Chapter XI

*T*he two weeks leading up to Christmas were a surreal and quiet time for Samantha. Agents were already on vacation, if not in reality, than at least in their minds. Although she had eight outstanding queries and a few manuscript submissions, her mailbox and e-mail inbox were devoid of responses. Craig and his agent were finishing the final touches on his edits at the publishing house. He pitched the work of his second novel to them as well, which landed him a celebrated two book deal. His promised delivery was early spring on the second manuscript, so when he wasn't working on the edits of the first, he was busy writing the second. Samantha was nearing completion of the first draft of her second book as well, which pleased her since the first one had taken so long to write.

"I was writing after work and on weekends, which really slowed the process down. I love doing it this way so much better," she told Craig. "I can keep writing and not have to go back and re-read the chapter leading up to where I left off a week ago or even a few days ago.. But this, this is the way to write. Stream of consciousness. Love it!"

They were lying in bed on a Wednesday morning as Raindrops struck against the window panes before crawling their way down to the sill. The comforter covered everything except their heads and Craig's left foot, which hung out over the edge. Samantha lay with her head on his chest, playing with its tuff of hair; She noted a few gray ones. When she looked up at him, his chin and jaw line bore the beginnings of a five o'clock shadow. *Must be five o'clock in the morning shadow*, she thought. Beneath the covers they were wrapped in one another, waking from a night of love making. They were discovering new pleasures with one another each time, and the way they felt for each other remained indescribable.

Although they had awoken, the alarm had yet to go off. Samantha leaned up on her elbow and looked over Craig's shoulder at the clock that was flashing 12:00 a.m. across the display.

"Ohmygod, the power must've gone out during the night," she said and looked down at her watch. "Crap, it's eight o'clock already!"

"Do you have somewhere you need to be?" Craig pulled her back down next to him.

"Well, no," she admitted.

"It's okay to sleep in once in a while. You work on your books everyday; you're entitled to a breather. In fact, it's good for you." The soft tips of his fingers ran along her cheek as he spoke.

"You're right. Sometimes I feel so pressured against time to sell my book. To know I'll be okay. That I made the right decision." Samantha repositioned herself on his chest, needing the comfort, needing to feel safe in her world. It wasn't often that she doubted her decision because she was normally so busy writing and didn't have time to think about it.

"Don't feel guilty. There's no reason." They lay in silence until Lunar let out a whimper from the floor at the foot of the bed. "Now there's a reason to get up," Craig said. "I'll go let her out, you stay here where it's warm."

Samantha heard Craig's footsteps as they went down the stairs, followed by Lunar's paw-pattering. Knowing she had a few minutes, she grabbed her journal and wrote,

> *Craig eases my worries. He*
> *calms me, and he's simply good*
> *for me. I am so lucky to have*
> *found him. Although, he would*
> *argue that he found me first.*

She tucked the journal back in its place and nestled back under the covers, falling into a restful state...not sleep, but serenity.

*****

Christmas Eve was two days away and Samantha still hadn't finished her shopping. She sent gifts to her family with a card apologizing for not being there this holiday season, but let them know she was doing well. *Better than I've ever been.* Over the phone they accepted that she wasn't visiting for the holidays, but most of their acceptance because Craig was in her life. They still saw her as a woman who needed to be taken care of by a man, especially if she was going to continue her "hobby" of being a writer. Samantha learned to ignore the underhanded comments and to limit the information she gave them. Somewhere along the line she told them she was looking for an agent, as that was a necessary portion of the process, but never told them more than that. The less she told them, the fewer questions she'd have to answer later. *"Did you hear back from that agent? Where were they? Ohio?"* she imagined. On the contrary, by her not divulging information about her life, it made them think she was sleeping in until nine every morning and that she was living the life of leisure. They never asked about her finances, and Samantha didn't offer information either. The more reasons she gave them to worry, the more stressful it was on her. Occasionally Samantha's sister asked round about questions, but she always diverted the subject. Lunar needing to go out or be fed had become her standard excuse to end the call. Just as she did with phone calls, when she mailed the gifts and cards, she offered holiday wishes and kept it at that.

Amanda and Craig were different. She wanted to go all out for them...best friend and boyfriend titles didn't do them justice. For Amanda she picked up a gift certificate for a day at the spa on the outskirts of town—a full hour Swedish massage, pedicure, manicure, wraps, the whole package. Amanda wasn't one to pamper herself, but when others offered it to her, she more than obliged. The new Snow Patrol CD was added to the gift list too. Those two items and a card finished Amanda's presents. Craig was another story. *What do you buy for a boyfriend that you haven't said "the three words" to yet, but feel it and know he does too?* A serious and special relationship deserved more than a DVD and a flannel shirt. She did, however, pick out a thick, black cable sweater at Banana Republic for him. He looked great in black and the turtleneck would accent his jaw line. But, her main gift for him would be truly special.

"Where do I find truly special?" she asked Amanda.

"Geez, you had to wait until two days before Christmas to find *truly special*? Okay, let's think. You're both writers, so obviously something that reflects that would work. What about a new computer bag? You could have it monogrammed if you hurry."

"That's not special," Samantha said, chewing on her nails.

"Well, there's that stationery store on Pleasant Street. Try going there, at least it might spark something."

"*There*, now that's a good idea."

The sales woman at the store approached Samantha.

"May I help you?" she asked in her best perky, but soft/librarian? voice.

Samantha looked around the store — walls and shelves covered in pastel, bright, and contrasting colors. Envelopes, sheets of papers, stickers, notebooks. It was all so girly.

"What do you have, if anything, as a gift for a man?"

"Well, let's see. Over here we have some leather attaché cases. They come in scrumptious shades of browns and reds, or you can go with classic black." The sales woman unraveled her arm toward the cases, her best Vanna White impression.

"Not personal enough, I'm afraid." Samantha said more to herself than to the woman.

"Well, how about a pen? We have all sorts and you can have it engraved. The display case is over here." The idea of the pen was simple, but the engraving intrigued Samantha enough to follow the woman. The glass case was filled with wide, narrow, wood, and metal pens. The pen would have to come in a beautiful case. There were three that caught her eye as being masculine enough for him. "What does he do?" the woman asked.

"He's a writer. Mystery. Can I see this one, and the one above it," Samantha asked. "Oh, and the one in the back row, it's black."

"A writer, how exciting. Let me pull these out for you."

The three pens were placed side by side on a velvet mat atop the glass. Immediately, Samantha ruled out the one on the right. It didn't look as exquisite. Narrowing her selection down to the one in the center and the one on the left, she picked up the middle one first. It was a dark blue, metallic pen and the weight of it was substantial. When she gripped it, the thickness of it felt right. Then again, Craig's fingers were barrels compared to her sinewy ones. She'd have to imagine how it would feel in his grip.

The second one, a mahogany stained wood, had less of a curve to it. The wood against her fingers felt warmer than the cool metal of the first, but it also felt as though it was absorbing moisture from her skin. Finicky, she knew, but it just didn't feel like something that she'd want to hold for a long time. Yes, Craig used his laptop for his writing, but when he went back to edit his work, he printed the script and did a hard-copy edit with pen to paper — as did she. The old-school red pen wasn't needed, but the pen she selected had to be one that he'd want to hold for hours. If even it lay upon his lip as he read, and only occasionally touched the page, it would remain in his hand. Deciding on the metal one, she asked the woman if it came in black.

172

"Yes, it does. I'll need to go in back and find one for you."

The woman disappeared to the storeroom, leaving Samantha to consider an inscription. She hadn't had time to think about that since the concept hadn't entered her mind until it was suggested. She toyed around with his initials, both of their initials, and "Christmas 2006," but none of those were right. It had to be words. "Writer's do it between the covers" came to mind...she laughed and thought that although it was fun, it wasn't sentimental enough. "Lattes with Love" was a thought, since it was where they met, but she knew there was something better, and as a writer, she should be able to find the words.

Samantha walked over to the window and looked down the street. The coffee shop was on the corner, barely in view. Samantha thought about her life before Craig and how she had learned to be happy right before meeting him, unlike when she met all of the others. It wasn't because of him that she was content, yet he was the beneficiary of her new found persona, and maybe that's why they seemed to work.

The woman returned and presented Samantha with the black, metallic pen.

"It's perfect. Can you hold onto it for a few minutes while I run next door?" Samantha asked. She wanted to go in the neighboring bookstore. In their late night talks, Craig often quoted Buddhist philosophies, which intrigued Samantha due to her new found thought process and positive outlook on life. She often felt as though she could convert to Buddhism quite easily and had spent some time researching the theories on the internet during her breaks at the coffee shop. The Eight Fold Path and the Four Noble Truths were concepts that she was striving to live by and many of her discussions with Craig fell under these beliefs. Hence, she wanted to find a book with an appropriate quote that would pertain to them and also reflect the philosophies that they both shared.

Nirvana in and of itself wasn't enough, she thought. There had to be a few more words. A few minutes later, she was standing in the bookstore, staring at a shelf full of Buddhism books, the inscription came to her. "Writing is Nirvana." The scope of its meaning was far reaching for them, unimaginable by others. Just what she wanted.

The sales woman holding the pen for Samantha took the meaning on its surface layer, "That's a nice idea, dear," and that's when Samantha knew she made the right decision. She was told she could pick it up the next morning and the inscription would be done. After paying for the pen, Samantha was relieved to have found the perfect gift. While she was in town, she stopped into Lattes with Love for her usual. It was a quiet mid-afternoon crowd. Christmas music played in the background and mistletoe hung in the doorway. While she was waiting for her latte, her phone rang. Retrieving it from the depths of her purse was a challenge, and when it finally emerged it displayed an unfamiliar area code. "Hello?" she said, stepping away from the speaker above her that sang out "Deck the Halls."

"Hello, is this Samantha Sounder?"

"Yes, this is she." The woman's voice was friendly and professional. Not a collector.

"This is Katie Gary, Dr. Whitmore's sister."

Samantha's knees started to give out from under her; she found a seat to sit in. "Yes, hi. How are you?" She didn't know what else to say until Ms. Gary let her know why she was calling.

"I'm doing fine. I wanted to talk to you because I'm in the car with my husband heading down to my brother's for the holidays. I'd like to meet with you while I'm in town. I cleared my schedule for a few days after Christmas. Will you be around?"

"Um, yes, yes I will be." Samantha looked outside the window at the cars passing by, not knowing what else to do. *An agent calling me? Wanting to meet me?* She never expected to hear from an agent so close to the holidays.

"Great. How does the afternoon of the twenty-sixth sound? We can meet at a coffee shop. Isn't there a Starbucks or something?"

175

"Actually, there's a quieter one called Lattes with Love on Main Street. I can meet you there."

"Oh yes, I remember that one. Fine. Let's say three o'clock."

"Great. I'll meet you here. Uh, there." Samantha said, expecting to hear a click.

"Oh, and Samantha."

"Yes?"

"I loved reading *Winter's Truth*. Be prepared to sign a contract if you're interested."

"Okay. Thanks for letting me know! I'll see you on the twenty-sixth." Somehow anything else didn't sound right. She was grateful that Ms. Gary hadn't left her hanging through the holidays.

"Medium latte," called the teenager behind the counter.

Samantha stood up to pick up her latte, which she no longer really wanted. All she wanted was to run and find Craig to tell him about Ms. Gary. On the street she sat down on a bench and looked at the sky. "Thank you!" she said out loud to the Universe. "Thank you!"

Every ounce of her being radiated joy, relief, and satisfaction. The biggest hurdle was met. She had an agent. Well, she hadn't signed yet, but Ms. Gary said to be prepared to and that was good enough for Samantha. Placing her latte on the seat of the bench, she retrieved her cell phone from the bottom of her purse where it had sunk back in somewhere after she hung up with Ms. Gary and picking up her drink at the counter. Craig's phone rang and between the second and third rings, Samantha said, "C'mon, hun, answer the pho-"

"Hello?"

"Ohmygod! You're there! Guess what?" Samantha stood up, her purse falling to the ground.

"Wow, you sound excited. I give up, what?"

"Katie. She called! She wants to meet on the twenty-sixth. She wants to sign me! Me! She wants to sign me! Can you believe it?"

"hun, that's fansupertastic! I'm so happy for you. Seriously, do you have any idea how happy I am for you?"

"No. Tell me. Pinch me. I can't believe this!"

"Where are you? I'll come meet you. I was just about to head out anyway."

Samantha looked at her watch. Five o'clock. "I'm at the coffee shop of all places. She called just after I ordered my latte. How cool is that?" A man in a gray suit walked by and pointed at her purse sitting on the ground, barely beneath the bench. She nodded at him and reached down to retrieve it. "I'm going to run an errand, but I'll meet you back here in twenty. Does that work?"

"Perfect. Can't wait." Craig hung up and Samantha scooped up her latte, purse back in her hand, and went back to the stationery store.

"You're back," the woman said. She was cleaning the glass where the pens were encased.

"Yes. I'd like to buy another one of those pens, please. Except for the second one I'd like red, but with the same inscription."

Samantha's determination in her voice did not go unnoticed.

"Sure. They will both be ready tomorrow morning. You can pay for the second one then if you'd like."

"Perfect. Thanks," she said and strolled back onto the sidewalk. *Amanda! I have to call Amanda.*

"Hey, Sammy. Whassup?" Amanda said when she answered.

"Everything. Everything's up. Guess what?"

"Craig proposed! Ohmygod!"

"No. Not that. Better. I think, anyway." Samantha took a sip of her cooling drink.

"You sold your book!"

"Well, close. I landed an agent! The vet's sister. Katie. She's coming down for the holidays and wants to meet me. Can you freakin' believe it?"

"Woo-hoo! Way to go Sammy! I knew you'd do it. I just knew it!" Samantha could hear Amanda jumping up and down through the phone.

"I'm still in shock. It hasn't sunk in."

"Did you call Craig? He should propose to you now because you're gonna be a rich, famous author!" Samantha laughed at that one.

"Amanda, don't go putting ideas in his head. He has his own books anyway. I'm just so relieved. This was a huge hurdle to get over and it's done. He's on his way to meet me so I've gotta run. I'll keep you posted though." Samantha hung up and made her way back to Lattes with Love where she sat back down on the bench outside. Although it was only in the fifties outside, she didn't want to go indoors. She wanted to see Craig as soon as he arrived, and when he did, she flew into his arms the minute he shut his car door. He swung her up into the air, catching her in his arms, her legs wrapped around his waist. They locked into a long kiss. No words were necessary. He was proud of her, relieved for her, and excited for both of them.

"I'm taking my girl out to dinner. Where do you want to go? Anywhere. It's your night." He looked into her eyes and added, "I'm so proud of you. So happy for you. You deserve this."

Samantha's eyes welled up and she choked out, "I know. I do deserve this, don't I? Thank you for-"

"Oh no – this was all you. I didn't do anything."

"Yes you did! If it weren't for you I wouldn't even know I needed an agent!"

"Ah, you would have figured it out," he said.

Samantha tucked her head down and kissed him.

"Maybe. But I still couldn't have done it without you." He kissed her back.

"Now, where to?"

Samantha suggested the Thai restaurant they went to on their first date, and since it was right around the corner they were able to walk. Craig let her down from his clutch, but grabbed hold of her hand.

"You're beautiful when you're happy," he told her as they walked side by side.

"You're handsome when I'm happy," she giggled. He reached his arm around her waist and pulled her in close to him.

Chapter XII

*I*n the wee hours of Christmas morning, Samantha woke up in the middle of a dream. The warmth of Craig's body next to hers matched the serenity of the dream. A small rowboat floated down a river. The riverbank's trees and shrubs passed by methodically, plenty of spots to pull over in the boat. The paddles slapped the water, spun underneath the current, and pulled back up, rhythmically, peacefully. The last slap of the paddle that pushed the boat to shore woke Samantha up, making her check her face for the splashed water.

The moonlight through the blinds was dim. Craig's breathing was steady. Lunar's too. Samantha let the memory of the dream flow through her mind—she closed her eyes again and allowed it to come back. The rowboat was wood with metal trim. She wasn't sure who was paddling it, but she sat in the middle and watched the scenery. She wore a long, flowing skirt with a floral print and a white spaghetti strap tank. Long gold earrings shaped like a teardrop hung from her earlobes, each one punctuated with a diamond. In her hands was a book. Transferring her mind deeper into the memory of the dream, she realized it is her book. It is published. She took the memory to the shore where she landed and woke up. No rough, tumultuous water.

Craig rolled over, flopping an arm across her belly. She laughed quietly and took hold of his hand, gently raising it to her lips and let it rest there, her warm breath against his palm. He didn't wake and she lowered the weight of his hand back to her belly, the rhythm of her breathing raising and lowering it still. She fell back to sleep thinking that this was already the best Christmas.

*****

"Merry Christmas, hun," Craig said, waking Samantha for the second time that morning.

"Merry Christmas to you," she replied, reaching for his hand and finding it where she had left it only a few hours ago.

"You wait here. I'll be right back," he said and slowly released his hand from its position as though it might hurt her by doing so.

"Where're you going?"

"You just wait here. I'll let Lunar out and we'll be right back up," he said, shooting her an innocent smile over his shoulder as he made his way through the bedroom door to the hallway, Lunar in tow.

Samantha rolled over to his side of the bed, absorbing the heat he left on the sheets, his smell. It wasn't long before he returned.

182

"Close your eyes!" he said, peeking his head around the corner and into the room. "Are they closed?" he asked.

"Yes, they're closed. Promise!" Samantha said. all she heard were his footsteps approaching. Giggling, she covered her eyes in an attempt not to peek.

"What is it? It's not alive is it?"

Craig laughed, "No, it's not alive. Open your eyes."

When Samantha opened her eyes she was faced with a stocking as big as Lunar. It was stuffed, brimming with goodies.

"Oh my! You didn't have to do that!" She sat up next to Craig. "But, I'm glad you did."

Next, Samantha lay down over the edge of the bed and pulled a stocking out from underneath. "For you!" she told Craig. They kissed good morning said Merry Christmas once again. The next hour was spent opening their stocking presents and giggling over the silly gifts they bought each other. Lunar delighted in the rawhide bone and squeaky toys that Craig gave her.

Samantha leaned up against her pillows, legs stretched out in front of her with her feet tucked under Craig's thigh. She watched as he opened the last present in his stocking, a coffee mug with Lattes with Love's logo on it.

"I wondered what was so heavy in here," he said. "How 'bout I go put some Joe on?" Craig said. He kissed her on her forehead, stood up and opened the blinds, then made his way downstairs.

"I'll have tea. There's some raspberry in the cabinet," Samantha called to him.

Samantha hopped into the shower and changed into a pair of jeans and a sweater before going downstairs. In the living room, the walls glowed with the reflection of the tree's lights. Lunar lay next to the couch chewing on her toy, and Craig was in the kitchen cooking eggs. Standing on the bottom step, Samantha took a mental picture of the scene in front of her, never wanting to forget it. Presents were piled up underneath the tree, and Craig had hung their emptied stockings over the fireplace where he had also lit a fire. It dawned on her as to how much he had done while she was merely in the shower and getting dressed.

She felt the cold kitchen floor on her bare feet as she walked over next to Craig. The sink was filled with a dirty pan and utensils.

"Mmm. That looks good," she said hovering over the two plates of eggs and toast.

"The final touch," Craig said as he added a dash of paprika to the top of the eggs. "There, now we can eat. Go ahead and have a seat. Your tea is on the table," he kissed her and shooed her away. "Do you want some orange juice too?"

"Sounds perfect," Samantha said, stopping in the hallway to put on her slippers.

Craig carried the two plates over the table. Two glasses of orange juice followed, and then he sat down. Holding his own glass of orange juice up, he toasted "Merry Christmas" to Samantha.

"You have no idea," she said. "No idea how merry this Christmas is."

"Are you ready for your big meeting tomorrow?" Craig asked and took a bite of egg.

"I guess so. I've done all the hard work having written the book. Now I just need to sit back and listen to what she has to say," Samantha said. "This is good." She held a forkful of egg up to him.

"Make sure to read over the contract very closely. They're all pretty standard at fifteen percent. I don't think she's dishonest at all, it would just be good for you to understand it as well as you can."

"I'll have her explain it to me. That's what she's there for," Samantha said. "I'm sure she has it down pat. I'm still pinching myself. When I woke up this morning I instantly remembered a dream I had."

"Was I in it?"

"I dunno. I was in a rowboat floating down a river. Everything was peaceful and calm. I don't know who was rowing it. I only saw the paddles. I don't think it was you. Sorry. I think it was a supernatural force."

185

"Hey, I'm a force to be reckoned with," Craig teased.

"You know what I mean. Not a living being, but a universal being. Spirit like."

"Sounds like a terrific metaphor for your life right now."

When they finished eating, Samantha insisted that she do the dishes and that he relax on the couch. After washing the pan and rinsing the utensils, she moved onto their plates, which would go in the dishwasher. Pausing, she watched Craig from the kitchen as he sat on the couch engrossed in a magazine article. A thick lock of black curl rested on his forehead over his left eye. Long legs extended the length of the couch and his broad shoulders took up most of the width. Turning to finish the dishes so that she could join him, she thanked the Universe for bringing her such a lovely and loving man. *I know it sounds corny,* she thought to the Universe, *but he's the one. I can't believe I'm admitting it, but he's the one.*

Water flowed over the last dish, washing off the crumbs until it was clear and placed in the lower rack. Samantha joined Craig on the couch, curled up in his arms, legs stretched out next to his, she nestled her head in his neck while he finished reading the article.

"Ready for presents?" he said a minute later.

"Presents? Did you say presents?"

186

The tree was only a few feet away, and most of the presents were in reach. Craig leaned over and picked one up for Samantha.

"Who's this for? Me or you?" she asked, holding up the pink Victoria's Secret silk nightgown that she pulled out of the box. Craig grinned and raised his eyebrows in classic male hubba-hubba fashion.

He opened the black turtleneck sweater and made a joke about it being warmer than the nightgown. After a few fun, informal gifts, Samantha handed Craig a small, thin box.

"Pretty short for a tie," he said. When he tore the paper off, he looked at her in wonderment. The leather case had his initials across the top, and when he opened it, two pens lay side-by-side—her red one and his black one. He lifted the black one out of the case and read the inscription.

"This is amazing," he said.

"The red one is actually for me. Kinda his and hers, but they both have the same inscription. I thought you could use a good pen for all of your book signings."

Craig held up the red one up, next to his.

"They're perfect." He leaned over and took her in his arms. "Now for you," he said, pulling a box out from under the cushion and handed it to her.

"Ohhh. I like little boxes." Peeling the tape off of either end, Samantha gently unwrapped the package, treating it as a delicacy. Her hand trembled as the wrapping paper fell to her lap and she lifted the lid of the black velvet box that exposed the most beautiful pair of diamond earrings. "Oh...my...god." The words slid slowly off her tongue. "They're exquisite!"

One by one she picked them up and held them out before her, awed by their beauty. "I can't believe you did this. Thank you." She leaned over and embraced him. "You're amazing. They're amazing."

"I figured you'd need a nice pair to wear to your contract signing tomorrow."

"Oh, you can bet I'll be wearing them.
Tomorrow and each day after. They're gorgeous." Samantha reached up to her ears and put the first stud in, then the second. She leaped off of the couch and ran to the hallway mirror to have a look.

"I love them!" she exclaimed; the shock was wearing off and excitement had kicked in.

Samantha ran back to couch and leaped into Craig's arms. She wrapped her arms around his neck and looked him right in the eye. "Thank you. Not just for these, but for being you and being in my life."

"I love you," he said.

"I love you too. Have for a while now."

"Me too."

The couch absorbed their bodies, and Christmas morning was soon over. By afternoon, they settled into reading, watching television, and phoning family and friends. Samantha called Amanda first. "Wait till you see them. They're stunning. I think I've used every synonym for beautiful to describe them!"

"Oh Sammy, you've found a winner. He's a keeper. Can't wait to get back to town in a few days. Are you two still going to the New Year's party?"

"You betcha. I'll have a lot to ring in the New Year with. Call me when you get home." Samantha hung up with Amanda and called her family. She let them know about the earrings, but didn't want to say anything about Ms. Gary until the papers were officially signed.

By dinnertime, Samantha and Craig were fully ensconced in Christmas and hungry for the turkey dinner they spent the afternoon preparing. That night, Craig waited patiently in the bedroom while she was in the bathroom washing her face and brushing her teeth. When she emerged from the bathroom and towards him, his eyes widened at the sight of her in the pink silk nightgown. The spaghetti straps accentuated her lengthy arms. She turned around, her long dark hair flowing with the gown.

"So?" she asked, facing him again.

"So...that looks amazing on you. I knew it would."

She joined him in bed and they made love until after midnight when they finally collapsed into a deep, naked sleep.

Chapter XIII

*L*attes for Love's tables were a dark, honey-stained wood. A thick layer of shellac coating protected each one from coffee mugs and utensils, pens and laptops. Samantha thought three o'clock would never arrive, and if it came close, the clock would skip right over to the four and the signing with Ms. Gary would merely be a mirage. But, at two forty-five when Ms. Gary walked through the door, the mirage became a reality.

Samantha had found a quiet table. She wore brown suede pants that hugged her hips nicely and an oatmeal cashmere top that hung somewhat loosely around her neck. Her diamond earrings sparkled on each ear, and she chose not to wear a necklace. There wasn't one in her jewelry box that matched the earrings; it would have been like using plastic utensils with Waterford china.

Samantha waited to order her latte until Ms. Gary arrived. She didn't want to be half way done with one while Ms. Gary was just starting hers. She did, however, make sure there were no crumbs on the table, and that the seats were close, but not too close. She smoothed her hair with her fingertips, having worn it down she took extra care in blow drying that morning.

191

Clearly not a local, Samantha identified Ms. Gary the minute she walked in. Her platinum, shoulder length hair rested upon her Armani taupe colored pantsuit. Every spec of makeup was in place, gripping her skin. She was put together like you'd expect a New Yorker to be, yet with an added flare of her own. Quite possibly she tried to dress down a bit seeing as she was in the country, but clearly she wasn't from Westhall.

Samantha waved when Ms. Gary scanned the room. Spotting Samantha, she made her way over to the table. Samantha stood up and held out her hand.

"Ms. Gary? I'm Samantha."

"Please, call me Katie. It's so nice to meet you. Can I get you something to drink?"

Samantha hadn't thought about that. Should she let her pay? Deciding it could be insulting to not let her pay, she said, "Yes, I'd love a latte. I'll come up there with you. They know my usual."

When Samantha stood up, she discovered just how much she towered over Katie. At five foot eight, Samantha was taller than the average female, but she felt especially tall next to Katie, which on some level gave her the feeling of confidence and even power—not that she needed or wanted it.

When they returned with their drinks, Katie draped her Prada purse over the back of her chair and took a seat across from Samantha.

"So, your book," Katie started.

"Yes, my book. What did you think?"

While in line for the lattes, Samantha talked herself into relaxing and going with the flow. Katie was there because she *believed* in Samantha's book and there was nothing to stress about. The hardest part was over. Now, it was her time to radiate enthusiasm, something she would have to grow used to when it came to marketing the book.

"I think it's spectacular. The protagonist is loveable, laughable, and delightful. The audience will love her. They'll care about her, which is the goal. I only found a few editing issues that we can go over later." She stopped for a minute and retrieved her copy of the manuscript from her attaché case. "Now, I took the liberty of touching base with my top five editors to give them first dibs. I hope that was okay. I wanted to give them heads up before the holiday chaos. And with many of them taking vacation time now, it's a good thing that I did. Two requested the synopsis and the other three want the full. I'll send those out as soon as you sign on the dotted line." At this point, Katie raised her head from the manuscript and looked straight into Samantha's eyes. "I'm assuming, of course, that you're interested in signing with me?"

193

"Yes, absolutely interested. Can you tell me what all of that entails?" Samantha sat back in her seat a little, bringing her latte with her. She liked having the cup to hold, to ground her.

"I have the contract here, but let me go over it in layman's terms. This must all be new to you?"

"Yes. Admittedly, I only found out recently that I even needed an agent."

"Well that, my dear, is the first step that so many writers either don't know about or think they have the golden ticket to by-pass one." Katie placed the contract on the table in front of Samantha. "Here's your copy of the contract. I'll walk you through the highlights, then if there's anything you want to read in detail, you can. It's all very standard."

Katie continued to explain her fifteen percent fee along with the major facets of the contract. They discussed publishers, cover illustrators—including how she wouldn't have much say, if any, in that department, and marketing expectations. Samantha took notes on a pad of paper that Craig handed her after she kissed him good-bye. She asked Katie questions along the way, all of which were answered without hesitation. Samantha liked Katie's style; she was sharp, professional, but also enthusiastic about *Winter's Truth*. Katie mentioned a few of the other clients she worked with and that the agency was holding an open house in February that she hoped Samantha could make it to.

"You'll need to come to New York when an editor picks up the book. Sign contracts, smile, and all that. We'll need to find you a photographer for your headshot. You know, an author photo, for the jacket. Do you know anyone here?"

"No, I don't."

"That's okay. I have a list of them in New York. Set the appointment for late morning or early afternoon so you have time for the stylist. Let's see—" Katie looked down at the notes she came to the table with.

"What kind of advance do you think I'll get for this?" Samantha asked, surprising herself that she didn't whisper the question.

"Never can tell. I think it will be a good one, but it's up to the publishing houses. If more than one is interested, which I think they will be, it could go to auction."

"What does that mean?" Samantha's interest peaked.

"Interested editors will put in their bids until all others are outbid, just like a regular auction except it's usually done through phone and e-mails. That's the best case scenario."

"That sounds intense. I'd hate to ask what the worst case scenario is."

"Oh, I doubt you'll need to worry about worst case. You focus on marketing ideas, my dear. I'll take care of the editors."

Katie reached into her attaché case and pulled out her business card. "Howard and I need to head out. It's a few hour drive back to the city. Here's my card. My cell is on there. Call me anytime, and I'll let you know as soon as I hear something."

Samantha handed her a copy of the signed contract and stood to shake her hand. "Thank you so much. I'm so excited about this, but it's still all sinking in."

"All of my first time writers say that. It becomes less surreal when the money is in the bank and you're being whisked off to book signings. That's a ways away though. We'll do some small edits, do our best to find a publisher, then after that it takes about a year till the book rolls out. Part of that is because we send the book out to people to review it so that we can have reviews ready to go with the book."

"Oooh. That's cool," Samantha said.

"I've already toyed with ideas of a few other authors who would fit well with your book."

"I really appreciate all of the thought that you've put into this already. I feel as though I'm in really good hands."

"I have a reputation—you're in good hands. I'll be in touch."

Katie left with the same airy walk as when she arrived. Samantha sat down and held the contract out in front of her, then pulled it to her lips and kissed it.

"Thank you!" she said to the Universe, looking up at the ceiling. "Thank you!"

*****

The first snow fell the next morning. Craig was sitting at the kitchen table finishing his coffee and reading the paper while Samantha filled the dishwasher. The comfortable habit of his cooking and her cleaning began early on in the relationship.

"It's snowing!" Samantha announced from her spot at the window. She put the sponge down on the sink's edge and leaned in to see if it was sticking to the ground.

"So far it's sticking, but if it warms up, this'll be a mess. The flakes are huge. Come look," she turned to find Craig putting his paper down on the table and easing out of his seat. "Hurry," she said. "Big flakes never last."

Approaching where she stood, Craig wrapped his arms around her from behind, rested his chin on the top of her head, and gazed out of the window.

"You're right. Those are big ass flakes," he said, squeezing her tight. "They don't usually last long, do they?"

"No. They're like a freak of nature when they're that large. They should be framed."

"I need to run into town and pick up a few things. How 'bout I get some wood for the fireplace? I'll be back in a few hours." Craig

197

turned her around, keeping her within his arms. "I want to go before this gets bad...if it does."

"A fire would be great. The pile of wood out there got wet when it rained last week; I didn't realize there was a hole in the tarp."

"I'll pick up another tarp then too." Craig kissed Samantha on the top of her head and went to put on his shoes and coat.

Samantha walked him to the door and gave him a kiss goodbye.

"See you in a bit," she said. She watched as he wiped the snow off his windshield, climbed in the car, and then made his way down the driveway. The magical large flakes already turned to specs by the time he too was a mere speck going down the road.

"Lunar, do you need to go out?" Samantha called. Seconds later Lunar rambled her plump body down the hallway and out the open door. She had grown a lot over the holidays and was pushing forty or so pounds. A true Labrador, she still looked very puppyish. Samantha closed the door while Lunar was outside to keep the warm air in and returned to the kitchen to finish the dishes. A nearly empty box of dish detergent sat under the sink, and when she picked it up, she wished she had asked Craig to pick up some more while he was out. There was just enough left for this load, but not another. The whirl of the machine kicked in when she swung the locking lever over and pressed the knob. After a quick wipe-down of the countertops she headed back to the front door to let Lunar in. When she opened the door, a layer of snow covered the porch, but Lunar wasn't there. Nor were her footprints.

"Lunar! C'mon back in, Lunar!" Samantha called. The lack of sound as the flakes landed on nearby trees, grass, and the rooftop stirred Samantha's gut. "Lunar!" she called once more.

No sight of the pup.

Samantha threw on her Uggs and a coat and closed the door behind her. Making her way off the porch and around the side of the house, Lunar was no where in sight. Samantha checked the ground for paw prints, but all she saw was a mix of leaves and snow, leaving no trace.

The backyard revealed the same empty sight, and Samantha began to panic.

"Lunar! Where are you? C'mon girl!" The trees that lined the woods' edge didn't reveal movement. Samantha listened for crunching of leaves, anything that would indicate movement other than her own. Only quiet answered. Samantha ran to the edge of the woods, trying to find a trail—any kind of trail—that she could follow, certain that Lunar was in there somewhere. While no etched trail existed, she made her way through the wider gaps of trees, over stumps and downed branches, alternating between looking ahead and looking down at the ground for safe footing. Her clogs weren't quite the right shoes for the woods with a partially open heel, but she didn't want to waste the time of running in to find her boots. The next call of Lunar's name resulted in a crunch of leaves nearby, but Samantha's hope was squashed as soon as a squirrel made its way across her path.

"Damn it, Lunar! Where are you? It's cold out here!" she called. Half crying, she wrapped her arms together in front of her and shivered.

Unfamiliar with the depths of the woods, Samantha hesitated going too far. But, the thought of Lunar running loose in them was daunting. After dodging piles of fallen branches and ducking under tree limbs, Samantha stopped to assess her current location. The brush surrounded her like a crowd in a mall at Christmastime. Every angle looked the same, and none were encouraging.

"Luuuuunnnnnaar!" Samantha called, her voice cracking midway. "Damn it," she swore when she got no response. She looked at her watch, almost an hour had passed, and decided that she should go home in case Lunar was sitting on the front porch. She turned around to walk toward the house. Then turned again. And again. Which way was the house? *Shit!* The leaves cracked like kindling on a fire beneath her shoes with each turn. Looking up at the sky for the sun's positioning proved fruitless because it was not only about high noon—as high as the sun was in December—but, she didn't know in which direction to go. All she knew was that the sun rose in the east and streamed through her bedroom window in the morning. But, that didn't help her place which direction the actual house was from where she stood.

A plane flew low overhead, drowning out any potential noise in the woods. She took another look around, trying to remember something, anything, about which direction she came from. A white rock rested up against a tree, prompting her memory. She walked over to it and positioned herself in the angle she would have first seen it in.

"Okay," she said to any squirrel or chipmunk who might be listening. "This is a start." Turning, she started walking, looking for other clues. A knob in one of the trees was familiar due to the pile of leaves hanging out of the hole, stuck together from recent rains. Snow was still falling, changing the scenery, but in one brief opening she spotted one of her footprints.

"Better. We're getting there." The process of finding her way out was met with impedances that were not considered when she headed into the woods. She had dashed in wholeheartedly looking for Lunar. But now the branches and careful footing only slowed her down.

201

The smell of smoke from a chimney caught her attention. At least that was reassuring. Her neighbors were quite spread out, but some were visible in the winter. The odor translated into the thought of warmth. She realized then that she hadn't shivered in a while; the angst of finding her way on top of the walking generated enough body heat.

Intimidated by the idea that she was as deep in the woods as she was, Samantha stopped and sat on a stump. Looking up at the trees, they continued to spiral, making her dizzy. She threw her head forward and planted it in the palms of her hands. Tears uncontrollably rolled down her cheeks, off the edges of her palms, and onto the ground below. *Where could she have gone? Why would Lunar run away?*

The thought of Lunar chasing a squirrel was considered, but really, how far would a squirrel go before it found its way up a tree and Lunar would give up? Samantha lifted her head and wiped the streaming tears off her cheeks. She took in the views from all directions and immediately ruled out the direction she had just come. That left three to choose from. Not the best odds, but it was all she had to go by. Before standing up, she listened hard for a clue, any clue, then said out loud, "Please, God. Find me a way back. Give me a sign that I'm heading in the right direction." Waiting for a moment proved no response. Standing up, she twirled around and added, "I'm not giving up! Send me a sign that I'm heading in the right direction!" she yelled. *"Anything!"*

Brrrrrrrrrrrrggggggg. The sound of a truck in the distance. It was apparently trying to make it up a hill on the slippery roads. Then she heard the sound of metal on pavement.

"A snow plow? You sent me a snow plow?"

She listened harder and figured out which direction the plow's noise was coming from. There was only one main road near her house where vehicles could drive.

"Keep it going," she said and broke into a run toward the sound of the engine and blade on pavement. The louder the engine noise became, the faster she ran.

Bursting out of the woods and onto the road, it took Samantha a moment to acclimate herself. A look to the left showed the intersection that she and Lunar had walked to several times, meaning the look to the right headed home and up the hill where the plow was likely to have been slowed. Evidenced by the scraped road, her deduction was correct. Once again, the boots proved difficult for making headway, only this time as a runner. She made it most of the way up the hill, leaving a quarter mile or so till home when she heard another engine behind her. A horn honked gently and when she turned, Craig pulled up next to her.

"What's going on? You must be freezing!" he said, his window going down as he called to her.

"Lunar. She's gone. I can't find her."

"Hop in!" He reached over and opened the passenger door. Samantha ran around the car and jumped in, only glancing for a second at the pile of goods in the backseat.

"I let her out right after you left and she didn't come back," she exhaled heavily between words.

"Okay. Warm up with the heater. We'll find her." Craig accelerated up the hill, leaving his window down and calling, "*Lunar!*" as he drove.

Samantha warmed her hands against the vent. When they pulled down her driveway, creating new tracks, he stopped yelling, parked and hopped out in one swoop.

"Where was she?" he asked.

"I dunno. I went back in to finish the dishes and when I came back she was gone. Simply gone. The snow hadn't fallen enough to make tracks. God, what if she doesn't come home?" The tears rolled down her cheeks, this time dripping off her chin. Craig put his arm around her.

"You go inside and get a jacket and boots," he said looking down at her shivering body.

"Warm up a bit. I'll keep looking. She may be close by again and will hear our voices."

Samantha did as he suggested, not knowing what else to do. "Okay, I'll be right out. Keep calling her!"

*****

Another hour passed and both of their voices were hoarse from calling Lunar's name into the cold, unwelcoming air. Samantha's emotions ranged from sadness to frustration one minute to anger or despair the next.

"It's okay, we'll find her." Craig did his best to console her.

"That little scutter-bucket. What if—"

"Hey, no 'what if's.' C'mon, let's go back inside and warm you up."

"If I'm cold, how do you think she feels?"

"I know you're worried, but right now you need to warm up. She's got her fur and she's probably chasing a bunny rabbit or something. She'll be warm enough." Craig led Samantha inside and filled the kettle with water. "I'll make you some tea."

Samantha sat down on the couch and pulled a fleece blanket over her. Fighting back the tears, she thought of things to say, but each one sounded discouraging. Reminding herself to think positively, she reformulated her thoughts, first in her mind, then to Craig.

"You're right. She does have fur. I forget that she is an animal. She knows where the house is since we've walked down the road plenty of times. She'll be okay."

Taking her cup of tea from Craig, she was able to smile and say thank you. Twenty minutes later they re-bundled up at the door. Samantha was tying her shoelaces when her cell phone rang. Stumbling with only one boot, she answered the phone on the fourth ring, "Hello?"

"Um, hi. I was wondering if you own a little black pup—"

"Do you have her? Do you have Lunar?" Samantha turned to look for Craig, holding her arm out to him. He rushed down the hallway in time to hear her say, "You do? Is she okay? Where are you?"

All of the earlier angst was gone.

"She's fine. A bit wet from the snow. She showed up on my doorstep scratching to come in," the woman said.

"Where are you? I'll come get her right away," Samantha only wanted one thing in that moment—to bring Lunar home.

"Over at 302 Maple. We're the third right after the sharp turn by Holden's Farm."

"Perfect. We'll be right there." Samantha hung up the phone to find Craig already opening the front door.

Half an hour later Lunar was sound asleep by the fire and Samantha and Craig were lying on the couch, entwined in one another.

"I don't ever want to lose her again," Samantha whispered while Craig kissed her forehead.

Chapter XIV

*N*ew Year's Eve came faster than Samantha could ever remember in past years. Amanda met them at the door, dressed in a black halter dress. Silver star earrings dangling on either side. Laughter flowed to the outside as she opened the door. Kicking residual snow from their shoes, Samantha and Craig made their way inside to join the party.

"Happy New Year, guys!" Amanda said, tipping her half full glass toward them. "Put your coats on the chair in the dining room and grab a drink."

A crowd was gathered in the living room where a fire was roaring, remains of Hors d'Oeuvres sat waiting for the next set of fingers, and plenty of seats were left for Samantha and Craig to use. Some guests sat on arms of chairs or couches, others on the floor up close to the fire, and the rest on chairs. Greetings and names were shared when Samantha and Craig entered with their wine glasses already in hand. They found a spot on the love seat near the fireplace, surprised that it was still available. *Had Amanda made sure?* Samantha wondered.

Stories of skiing trips made the rounds; everything from downhill to cross country to water came up. One way or another, almost everyone had a story to share. Amanda refilled some of the food trays, checked to make sure everyone had enough wine, and at one point actually sat for a few minutes. *That's Amanda – ever determined to please*, Samantha thought, *yet never letting anyone please her.*

Craig finished his first glass of wine before Samantha and went to the kitchen for a refill. He found Amanda hovered over the sink rinsing a plate when he entered.

"Hey, great party Ms. Hostess," he said.

"Oh, hi there. I heard about Lunar's escapade the other day. Geez what a scare!"

"Yeah, Samantha was pretty upset. She really loves that dog." Craig leaned against the counter and filled his glass with a chardonnay. He wore black trousers with a cream turtleneck and cranberry crewneck sweater that nearly matched Samantha's wool sweater dress. It hugged her figure, yet hung just right. She had gone on a small shopping spree during the after-Christmas-sales in celebration of signing with an agent. "She's so excited about signing with Katie. I really feel like this is going to be her year. Don't you?"

"Uh! It's about time," Amanda said. "That woman deserves all the riches in life. She's the best."

"Well, that's kinda why I came in here. I wanted to run something by you," Craig took a sip from his glass.

"Shoot. What's up?"

"I love Samantha more than anyone I've ever known. She is so special and she makes me feel like I'm on the top of the world when I'm with her. She radiates a warmth that I've never known until now."

"Awww. I love what I'm hearing. Keep going." Amanda took a sip from her glass. She put down the dishes, shut off the water and held on to every word Craig said.

He leaned over and looked toward the living room, looked back at Amanda and whispered, "I want to marry her."

Amanda gasped, throwing her hand to her mouth.

"Shhhhh." Craig continued, "My concern is that she has so much going on right now with the agent and book deal. I don't want to do too much at once, ya know?" Craig was still whispering.

"Ooooh. Gosh. That's a tough one. In some ways you might be right. But, I dunno. She's wanted this for so long. Not just to be married, but to someone like you. Do you have any idea what she's been through? Those jerks."

"No, not really. She doesn't talk about old boyfriends much," Craig confided.

"Well, all I'll say is that you make the white knight look like Darth Vader. She hit the jackpot with you, and the best part is that I can see that she's actually letting herself be happy. She's not afraid of losing you like the others."

"Wow. I had no idea. Well, some idea, but not really. So, what should I do?"

"Valentines Day. Do it on Valentine's Day." Amanda nodded her head, affirming her decision—clearly with the help of wine.

"Isn't that a bit hokey?" Craig wiped a crumb from his sweater.

"No, not when it's this romantic. This right. Besides, I really don't think she's expecting it at all. You haven't been together that long." Amanda turned to the oven and took a cookie sheet of pigs in a blanket out of the oven to cool.

"Okay. So how do I keep it a secret and not have her expect anything? I want to totally surprise her." Craig reached out to grab pig in a blanket and quickly retracted from the heat.

"Ouch!"

"Those are still hot, hun. Give 'em a minute." Amanda handed him a towel. "The way I see it is that she will be so caught up in the book stuff, she won't see it coming. I can promise you that." She reached down and scraped a sticky residue off the floor, and when she stood she exclaimed, "I've got it!"

"Shhhh," Craig held his finger to his lips.

"Sorry." Amanda lowered her voice and continued, "New York. Work it out with her agent under the guise of having to meet with the publishers. She'll likely have sold her book by then and a trip up there would be easy to scheme. It's perfect!" Amanda put her hand to

211

her chest, "Oh how romantic. A proposal in New York City!"

"Watch it Amanda. We might make a believer out of you yet!" Craig laughed.

"Believer in what?" Samantha entered the room, empty glass held out to Craig for a refill.

Amanda turned to her cooling pigs in a blanket, the smile on her face would have been a dead give away.

"Having a puppy," Craig rescued. "She was so swooned by our little Lunar story that I think we might just find a puppy here the next time we come over." Craig pulled Samantha into him and kissed her on the forehead. "Can I get you anything else?" he asked her and handed her the glass back filled with the same chardonnay.

"I actually wanted to see if there was something I can do to help. Amanda, there must be something?"

"Yes, dear. You can take this tray out and place it on the coffee table." Amanda handed her the fresh tray. "Oh, and bring back any empty ones."

Samantha did as asked and left the kitchen with a tray.

"Nice recovery," Amanda said.

"That was close. We better get back out there," Craig said and picked up his own wine glass.

Craig and Amanda returned to the living room and planted themselves back in their seats; him next to Samantha who had placed an empty tray on the buffet outside the kitchen door when she saw them coming, and Amanda on the arm of a couch.

By eleven fifty, everyone had had their share of drink and celebration and the ten minutes left till midnight was spent either watching the ball drop in Time Square on her big screen television, in the kitchen picking crumbs off trays, or staring at a watch. Samantha and Craig found a spot in front of the television and held hands as Dick Clark counted down the last minutes.

"Ten, nine, eight," the room counted in unison, "seven, six, five, four, three," Craig held tighter to Samantha's hand, "two, one! Happy New Year!"

Those with partners clutched, kissed, and embraced. Those without toasted glasses to each other. Amanda stood in the kitchen doorway and watched it all happen.

*****

New Year's morning was half over by time Samantha and Craig woke up. Too tired to do anything but strip and crash when they got home, they woke up to a pile of clothes trailing from the door to the bed. The only thing that sounded good to Samantha was a stack of pancakes at the diner in town.

"Call and make sure they're open," she called to Craig, toothbrush pressed against her teeth, but barely moving.

"Okay. Hold on," he called back from downstairs.

She finished brushing her teeth and when she felt brave enough, she looked in the mirror. There it was—the face of a hangover. "Good lord, that's not the face I left with last night, is it Lunar?"

Lunar thumped her tail on the bathmat.

"I know. I know."

Samantha started water in the sink, waiting a moment for it to warm up. Cold was tempting to wake her up, but she remained realistic—warm would sooth. The tube of Origins Foamy Face Wash sat next to the toothbrush holder. She squeezed out a dime sized amount and lathered it between her fingers. The combination of water and froth rinsed away much of the bad juju from the night before.

"They're open. I made you a cup of tea to start with though," he placed the mug on the bathroom counter. "How do you feel?"

"Better now." She toweled her face dry and raised the tea to her lips. "Thank you. It's perfect."

The diner was busy when they arrived, but they only had to wait five minutes before being seated. "I know what I want," Samantha told the waitress who was pouring their glasses of orange juice. "But, let's give him a minute."

Craig held up the menu. "Well, I thought I wanted pancakes, but that Texan omelet looks

214

really good. I will need a minute," he said to the waitress.

While Craig mulled over the menu, Samantha watched his eyes, his mouth, marveling over the way she was starting her new year. New man, new agent. What else could she want? She couldn't think of anything. The rest, selling her book, was obvious.

"Any new year's resolutions?" she asked after he finally decided on the omelet.

"Just one," he said.

"Oooh. Do share."

"To make you happy."

"Well, that's no fun. You do that already."

"Oh. Well, I guess I'll have to come up with something more challenging." Craig winked at her and called the waitress over. He ordered for both of them and when the food arrived, they ate in peaceful bliss.

"It's so nice to not have to send queries out anymore," Samantha said on their way home. Bellies satisfied and all other shops closed, they chose to go back to her house.

"Your apartment," she teased him, "is growing cobwebs."

"I can agree with that. Both of our agents are top-notch. It won't be long before the books sell. Hey, we should have a party at the house. What do you think? We can invite whomever you want to celebrate. Maybe Amanda will bake her specialty pigs in a blanket?"

"Now that's extravagant!"

"Between the two of us we must have enough people to invite for a real celebration."

"Sure we do." The list was made when they returned, and Samantha hung it on the refrigerator. "Let's look at the list everyday and picture the party until it happens," she said.

"Really? Okay." Craig ran his finger down the list. "I'm picturing it. This is cool!"

"Can I share something with you?" Samantha said, taking his hand in hers.

"Anything. You know that."

"Come upstairs."

"Now this I like!" Craig said.

"Ha ha. Just follow me."

When they entered her bedroom, Samantha asked him to sit on the bed. "I'm going to read you some excerpts from my journal, but first I need to explain."

"Okay," he lay back against the wall, hands clasped behind his head.

"Right before I met you I went through and re-read all of my journals. Page by page. All five of them from the past several years," she started.

"Sounds daunting. But, go ahead."

"Well, what I discovered was that during those years that I wrote in them, I was mostly venting. You know, complaining and faulting people. It was a real eye opener to see it that way."

Craig nodded at her to continue.

"That's when it hit me. I was continuing to create those same experiences over and over. Different people, places and times, but the experiences were the same miserable ones."

"Very introspective," he said and reached over, taking one of her hands in his.

"Well, it gave me a new idea. And that was to start writing only positive things in a brand new journal, hence the Positive Journal that I've created here." She held it up to him. "What I did was every night, starting before I met you, I would write something positive about my day or a about my future. At first it was difficult because I wasn't used to thinking that way. It's hard to find any good when your life is crashing down around you. But, I endured and soon it became easier and easier."

"What a great idea. You should share this with others."

"Well, that's not all." Samantha's eyes welled up and she choked out the next words. "Then I met you, and that's when I knew it really works. When I signed with Katie I knew it worked. Everything that has happened since I started doing this has created the life I've always wanted but had no idea how to create. It's like I thought my life into fruition. Does that make sense?"

"More than you know." Craig released her hand and wiped a tear from her cheek.

217

"Tears of joy. That's all I know now. I wish I had discovered this a long time ago, but I also know — we also know — that there's that timing thing. I wouldn't appreciate what I have now if I didn't have my old life to reflect on."

"This concept ought to be in one of your next books. Run it by Katie. Will you read some of it to me?"

Craig leaned back into his spot against the wall, closed his eyes, and listened to Samantha's soft voice read segments from the sprawled on pages. The words came through as those of intention, with no ego attached, and he was taken in by the promise they provided. She paused here and there, turning pages until she found another to share. Some he laughed with her, some drew a smile to his face, and others he nodded in agreement — those were the ones he opened his eyes for and looked into hers.

Samantha chose the best ones to read and with each, she could imagine the specific night that she lay in bed or on the couch to write them. The earlier ones showed the difficulties she had by changing her thought habits, her outlook on life. But by the middle she warmed up and the flow of the words etched with ease onto the pages. Her last entry from two days ago was the last one that she shared, "It all falls into place — doesn't it? When one not only believes in, but feels love, feels success, feels happiness. The Universe provides for us when we are in alignment with the gifts that we are asking for. I wish for everyone to learn this. To know this. To feel this. In reality, the Universe is My Sugar Daddy."

"Oh, now that, I love! The Universe is your sugar daddy. That's perfect." Craig sat up, taking Samantha and the journal into his arms, against his chest, and tucked his chin on top of her head. "I love you. Ya know that, don't you?"

"I sure do." Samantha turned her head up and met her lips to his. The journal fell by the wayside and they made love for the rest of the afternoon.

Chapter XV

*K*atie's voice on the other end of Samantha's phone became a regular occurrence by the middle of January. On the 19th Katie sounded different. Ever the serious New Yorker, Samantha heard elation for the first time. "Samantha, this is Katie. We've got an auction!"

"What? You're kidding, right?" Samantha was in the kitchen making a grocery list while Craig was reading on the couch. He stood up and came by her side.

"Three editors want it. I've been e-mailing and phoning back and forth with them. Be ready to come up here. I'm sure we'll have a decision in the next few days."

"Yes. Ohmygod! Yes. I'll be there." Samantha leaned against the counter, one hand holding her phone, the other gripping Craig's arm. Katie went on with the details, each one flew by Samantha who was still replaying the first words Katie said over in her mind. *An auction*? When there was silence on the other end, Samantha asked, "Could you e-mail me details so I can print them out?"

"Already on my to-do list. I'll have it to you this afternoon. Congratulations, Samantha. This is just the beginning." Katie hung up, as she rarely actually said good bye.

The phone, fused to Samantha's hand, went quiet.

"My book. She's got it going in an auction," she told Craig as though hearing it out loud would make it real to her. "I can't believe it." Her voice was soft, almost confused. "It's what I wanted and it's happening. It's all falling into place. I knew it would. I've been waiting for this, but now that it's here it doesn't feel real."

"It'll feel real when you sign the publisher's contract! Samantha, this is so fabulous! I'm so happy for you!"

"My god. They're fighting over my book!"

Craig swooped her up in his arms, holding her above his head then slowly lowering her till their faces met.

"I'm so proud of you," he followed with a kiss. "We're gonna hit New York City! It's going to be amazing. Magical."

"Maybe you can meet Roger for lunch while we're up there," she said.

"That's a good idea. He might regret taking me on when he could've had a star like you," Craig tugged at her shirt and flashed a wide smile at her.

"Oh please. He could sell your book in one swoop for a lot more than mine might make at auction. Just never know."

"Listen to the expert, ladies and gentlemen. Samantha, our literary specialist has spoken!" He swooped her up again; her legs swung around him and tightly gripped his waist, clasping her feet behind him he lowered her onto the couch, both of them in hysterics. Lunar jumped up, licking their faces until Samantha had tears rolling down her cheeks from the laughter.

*****

Craig treated Samantha to a train ride into the city instead of driving since it was more relaxing. He made reservations for a deluxe room on the 33rd floor of the Four Seasons Hotel, asking specifically for one overlooking Central Park. Walking through the lobby between the pillars and up to the check-in desk, Samantha took in the riches. A woman in a black leather coat tied tightly at her waist brushed past them as she barked orders at whomever was on the other end of her phone that her car must be in front by the time she exited the hotel. Samantha was amused by the woman.

After checking in, the bellhop took their bags and led Samantha and Craig to their room.

"It's all so decadent," she whispered to Craig from the corner of the elevator. He winked at her and the bellhop smiled.

The door opened to a king size bed and an even larger window with a view of the park, as promised. Although it was late January, Samantha still thought the view was beautiful. In an hour or so it would be dark and the light show would begin. Craig slipped some bills into the bellhop's hand and thanked him for his services. Once alone, they flopped down on the bed side-by-side and stared at the ceiling holding hands.

"Katie said it was just the beginning. What a way to start. This room is incredible. The views—"

"You're incredible. Remember that. You deserve all of this. All of it."

"All right. I know. It's still remarkable though." Samantha rolled off the bed and began to unpack some of her clothes that she didn't want wrinkled. "Hard to believe that this time tomorrow the auction will probably be over. I'll know what the world thinks *Winter's Truth* is worth."

"Yes, you will. What do you think for now…room service or eat out? How tired are you?" Craig unzipped his own bag, took out a charcoal gray suit and hung it in the armoire. Samantha hadn't answered him yet, as she had entered the bathroom where she stood, mouth agape, looking at the soaking tub, marble floors and countertops, and the glass doors surrounding the shower.

"Craig. Look at this!" When Craig joined her she said, "I'm thinking room service and a hot bath. What do you think?"

"Now you're talking decadent, my dear. I'll order. Why don't you change into something comfortable for dinner then we'll soak after we eat. You must be starving." Craig squeezed her shoulders and kissed her on the back of her neck. She nodded in agreement, retrieved her toiletries so that she could wash the travel grime off her face, and then changed into a pair of silk pajamas. It was early evening, but she knew they were in for the night and the pajamas felt right. Music flowed into the bathroom and when she walked out, Craig was lying on the bed reading a magazine.

The view had transformed to a dark palette speckled with dots of lights, mostly white. The curtains were pulled all the way to the sides. Standing in silence at the window overlooking the park, she took it all in, every bit of it. She wanted to remember everything so that she could tell her children and grandchildren some day...stopping herself, she realized that it had been a very long time since the concept of children entered her mind. When was the last time? When she was dating Robert? Had she seen her children in his eyes? Looking over at Craig now she understood the saying, "Thank God for unanswered prayers."

Fifteen minutes later, Craig answered the knock at the door and in rolled a cart with their dinner. Samantha disappeared back into the bathroom to touch up her makeup and run a brush through her hair while Craig situated the food and poured wine. They would have champagne the next night, which usually gave

Samantha a hangover, something she didn't want the coming morning.

They ate dinner, looking out at the city lights, chatting about their new lives as authentic writers. "I can't believe I am officially an author," she stated.

"Author?"

"Yes, author. A writer is someone who writes, like I used to be. But, to me anyway, an author has the connotation of being published. It's more official." Samantha stabbed at her salad, coming up with a chunk of tomato and a crouton dripping in oil and vinegar.

"Excellent point. I don't believe too many people muse over that one. That's what I love about you. You look at everything from all sides."

"Why, thank you," Samantha smiled at him. "I wonder how many famous writers— uh, authors—have stayed here. I'll bet quite a few. The view alone would bring in creative people, don't you think?"

"I wonder too. I'd bet more musicians than writers stay here. Just a guess, mind you. I don't have theories as brilliant as yours."

"Oh please. You're brilliant. And handsome. Did I tell you today how handsome you are?"

"No, not yet. But do, go on." He ran his foot up her calf under the table. "No, wait. Wait until we're in the soaking tub. That's

225

where I want to hear all about how handsome I am," he teased.

As advertised, the soaking tub filled within sixty seconds. The temperature was just right when Samantha dipped her toes in. The rest followed and Craig joined her a minute after she sat. She moved over and sat in his lap, both facing the same way, his arms wrapped around her.

"So, about my being handsome. Where were we?" Craig tightened his grip around her waist.

"Oh, yes. Let's see. I asked if I told you how handsome you were today, and you said to wait until we were soaking. So, here we are soaking, but I can't see you facing this way, so I'll have to go by memory." Samantha raised a finger to her mouth, pondering for a moment. "Those brown eyes and the way they light up when you see me. Now that's handsome. The way your turtlenecks ride along underneath your jaw line with an ever-so-slight gap between the two. Now that's just damn sexy." Samantha took a handful of water and dripped it on her shoulder, feeling the warmth roll down her blades and between their gap of their skin behind her. "The five o'clock shadow thing. Very hot. Especially the five o'clock shadow and it's in my bed. Yup. Hot."

"Hmmmm. Keep going. I like listening to this." Craig ran a washcloth along her shoulders, wringing it out on either side.

"Let's see. When you're reading a magazine or a book and you're really deep into it, your lip curls on the left side. Or is it your right?"

"You tell me."

"Your right, so my left when I'm looking at you. That's it."

Craig turned her toward him, stopping her words with his kiss. She pressed her bare breasts against his chest and wrapped her legs around him, a position that was becoming her favorite. They made love in the soaking tub, surrounded by marble, glass, and the music that continued.

Later, in bed, Samantha was back in her silk pajamas. Her cell phone rang and when she answered it, she received a full report from Amanda on the other end who was dog sitting Lunar. Samantha told her all about the room and the view.

"I feel like a princess. Next time you need to come. Maybe they allow dogs? I could walk Lunar in Central Park."

"Sammy, it sounds exquisite. Can't wait till tomorrow. Call me as soon as you hear something!"

"Will do. We're going to Serendipity afterwards to celebrate. I'll call you on the way."

"Have them interrupt me if I'm with a patient. I'll step out for a second. Don't forget and good luck! I love you guys! Have fun!"

Amanda hung up after promising to give Lunar the kiss that Samantha asked her to.

"Amanda sends her love," Samantha told Craig, who had his head back in his book.

"Great. How's Lunar?"

"She's fine. Amanda said she's letting her sleep with her tonight. I'm betting she'll have a puppy by springtime."

At ten-thirty they shut off the lights and crawled deep under the covers, wrapped in each other's arms. Facing each other, Craig brushed Samantha's hair off her forehead, kissed her goodnight and they fell asleep simultaneously.

Chapter XVI

*H*aving forgotten to close the curtains, the light streamed in early on Friday morning and woke Samantha up. Looking out to the sky above New York City was a first for both of them. After a quick breakfast, which Samantha was too nervous to finish, they made their way uptown to Katie's office. The secretary paged Katie, who arrived in the lobby dressed in a belted coffee colored sweater dress and a matching cream Pashmina. Her Prada bag clutched tightly under her left arm and her right hand pressed her cell phone against her face. She finished the phone call as she approached the glass door that separated the offices from the lobby.

"Samantha! Are you ready?"

"Most definitely. Katie, this is Craig. Craig, Katie," Samantha introduced. A shaking of hands went around the circle as Katie introduced her assistant, Zoe, whom, she explained, was fresh out of Columbia's MFA program and was working her way into the field.

Zoe pointed to the doorway and they followed in unison to a large conference room where they would wait and receive calls until the deadline of the auction. Samantha and Craig took seats next to one another and waited while Katie spoke to the editors one at a time, listening to their final bids. Zoe took notes and ran back and forth between Katie's office and conference room. Katie stood at the table to make her phone calls. Her fingers flew across the numbers on the telephone and when the first editor was on the line, she didn't waste time with chit-chat.

"What've you got for me? Got it. That's your final price?" Katie jotted a number down on her pad of paper, just out of Samantha's view. Craig squeezed Samantha's hand in his, sweat forming between the two. "Right. Sounds good. We'll let you know."

Katie hung up and dialed another number, clearly from memory, without looking up. "John? It's me. What've you got?" She held her pen to her lip and tapped her finger on the legal pad while awaiting his response. "I can hold." She turned to Samantha, "He's the last one. I'll go over all of this with you in a minute. Hang tight."

Samantha squirmed in her chair, knowing the offer can be anywhere from $5,000 to $1,000,000. She was beyond panic, beyond nerve-wracked. Having Craig next to her holding her hand eased her and knowing that this was the moment she worked so hard for, so long for. Her intentions would be met. All of her positive journaling would pay off. That was the point, wasn't it? To believe, to allow,

230

and to have unconditional faith that all would come to fruition in the perfect way. She thought about waking up next to Craig in their room at the Four Seasons overlooking Central Park. That moment alone was priceless—no matter what amount they put on her book, no one could put a value on her love for Craig.

"Okay, got it. I'll get back to you in a bit." Katie hung up the phone, made a few more notes and finally took a seat in the chair beside her.

"Well, my dear, you've got a decision to make!"

"Me?"

"Yup. There's a tie for the highest offer between Harcourt and Simon and Schuster. They're both offering five-hundred-thousand. The difference is that Simon and Schuster would make a two book deal."

"Five-hundred-thousand? Dollars?"

Samantha let go of Craig's hand and raised her own to her mouth. "Wow," she said under her breath. "And a two book deal?"

"Your option now is to decide which editor you think is right for you and for this book and whether or not you want to put in the second book." Katie went on to describe the two editors, their individual strengths. Samantha tried to absorb the data, but her mind was left back on the last zero of five-hundred grand. She hadn't known what to expect and purposely didn't try to put a number or expectation to mind, but this amount was life changing.

"Do you need a minute to think?" Craig asked her when Katie paused.

"Yes. Yes, I do." Samantha stood up and looked out the glass window of the conference room. It ran the length of the room and nearly the height. The view of towering buildings speckled with blue sky between each brought her back down to size. She suddenly felt small and put back in perspective. Was five-hundred-thousand a lot of money? Not to many of the people who filled the buildings before her. But definitely to the man on the corner selling pretzels, his hands gloved and kept warm by the heat of the pretzel oven. Samantha took a deep breath and returned to her seat.

"Katie, I trust your judgment. Which editor do you think would do the book the best justice?" Samantha asked. "Then again. I really can't turn down a two book deal either. This is what I've worked so hard for."

"Honestly, the editor at Simon and Schuster will do the book justice. The two book deal is golden...you know that. It's really not a hard decision, but it has to be yours.

"Okay. Craig and Katie, you're looking at a Simon and Schuster author!"

When the decision was made, Katie called the chosen editor to congratulate them on winning Samantha's manuscript and second novel. Hearing those words made Samantha feel on top of the world. She appreciated that so many editors were struck by her novel. Several months of stroking keys paid off and this was her moment to reap her rewards.

*****

"Serendipity," Samantha read from the screen of her computer, "is the act of finding something valuable or delightful when you are not looking for it." Samantha and Craig were back in their room at Four Seasons making phone calls and freshening up before going to Serendipity to celebrate. Craig was such a nervous wreck during the auction that he wanted to take a quick shower to rinse off his sweat and nerves.

"Serendipity is one of my favorite words; it just doesn't work in the thrillers that I write! *The killer serendipitously met his victim at her house.* Nope, doesn't cut it," he said.

"Ha. That's funny! Well, you should figure out a way to work it in sometime as a test of your writing abilities. Speaking of which, did you call Roger?"

"Yup. He'll be able to stop by between six and seven," Craig called to her from the bathroom. "I'm looking forward to seeing him again. Putting the face to the name as often as possible is always good. Besides, maybe some of Katie's good karma will rub off on him. He said he knows of her, but has yet to meet her."

The front of Serendipity, situated on East 60th street, was as quaint as Samantha had seen in pictures. Craig opened the door for her and they found Katie already at a table in the corner. Once seated, they started with appetizers and drinks while waiting for Zoe and Roger to join them.

"To *Winter's Truth*," Katie said, raising her glass to the center of the table. Craig and Samantha's glasses tipped in, clinking against Katie's. "I knew I was right to go with you. Five hundred thousand doesn't come along often. You're a very talented, but also a very lucky writer!"

"I feel comfortable with Kristin as an editor too. Out of all of them, she seemed to love the story the most. Enthusiasm goes a long way with me," Samantha said. "So, what's the next step?"

Katie went into the details of meeting with the publisher's cover illustrator who would be working on her book, the marketing department that will help devise a plan, and most importantly she would be in close contact with Kristin as they go through any edits.

"We can discuss your second book next week. *Fresh Fruit and Fresh Men*, I just love that title."

"Mmmmph," Samantha swallowed a bite of a honey wheat roll, "I'm just about done with the first draft."

234

"Might want to clean it up a little then send it along for feedback. I want to work closely with you on this one. Make sure it's tip top before we submit anything to Kristin. They want to know they got what they paid for." Katie raised her hand to the waitress to come over so she could order her clam chowder.

Zoe and Roger arrived within minutes of Katie's soup. The excitement level at the table rose to a new height.

"Katie, it's a pleasure to finally meet you," Roger said.

"Nice to finally meet you too. Looks like we have ourselves a dyno-duo here." Katie tipped her glass toward Samantha and Craig. Zoe had taken a seat between Katie and Samantha, leaving Roger next to Craig.

"Craig, good to see you again," Roger said. "And this must be your lovely lady, Samantha?" He extended his hand and gripped Samantha's in a man's shake. "You pick your ladies as well as you write your books!"

Laughter broke out around the table and once everyone was settled, the waitress came and took their orders. Through all of the commotion, Samantha caught Craig's eye and winked at him. For that moment in time, he was the only other one in the restaurant.

Samantha ordered the lemon chicken with a serendib salad and Craig ordered the steak. The chatter around the table would have given the impression that the five of them had been friends for years. Samantha noted the flirting going on between Katie and Roger. She pegged Zoe as a go-getter, but still naïve, who listened intently to the conversations and only pitched in when she was comfortable with her words. It was a mini-study in human character, a tool that Samantha had acquired since she started writing full-time. Some of her characters' personalities or quirks came from people she observed in the coffee shop. Now, sitting in New York City, she was presented with a myriad of characters to draw from—the waitress alone, she noted, contrasted drastically with the counter boy at Lattes with Love. She imagined the waitress as being the counter boy's mother who gave him up for adoption when he was five. Ideas for her third book were born during this visit to the city. She just hoped she'd remember everything. To take out a piece of paper and start writing or taking notes wasn't appropriate at this time. Instead, she excused herself from the table and went to the ladies room. After checking her makeup in the mirror, she took out her notebook and jotted down her thoughts. *A writer always writes.* She remembered having heard that somewhere. The simplest of truths. She filled almost a page of notes before returning to the table. Their dinners were being served as she took her seat.

236

"What did you do before you wrote your book?" Zoe asked Samantha.

"I was a Jill of all trades, but mostly functioned as an office manager. Well, at least I put on a good show," Samantha said. "Numbers were never my thing, and with all of the month end reports and balancing columns, it was a miracle when they were right. Thank goodness for software."

"I knew the minute I saw her that she was a writer. She has that look," Craig said.

"What look is that?" Katie asked him.

"Hot. Female writers are hot."

Roger laughed with Craig, and the women said, "Ahhhh."

Samantha was proud to have Craig by her side that weekend. Having someone like him to share her success with was so important to her. He took care of everything for them on the trip, freeing her up to enjoy the experience.

By ten o'clock Samantha and Craig excused themselves from the table, indicating that the excitement had exhausted them. Zoe had already left to meet some friends at Club 19. After shoulder-hugs with Katie, Samantha picked up her purse and took hold of Craig's arm. Roger promised to call Craig the next day when he was supposed to hear from two editors—finally promising news on his front.

As they walked out onto East 60th Street, Samantha's cheeks were pinched by the cold air. Newspaper and plastic wrappers swirled around their feet from the blustery wind. Craig wrapped his arm around Samantha and hailed a cab. The lobby was welcoming and the room even more so. Samantha didn't know that a bottle of champagne awaited their return to their hotel room—Craig had arranged it before they left.

"That was so much fun! What a way to celebrate," Samantha said and plopped herself down on the bed. She checked the phone on the nightstand for messages. No blinking light, but her cell phone showed three messages. She figured they were all from Amanda. Samantha had to leave her a message earlier with the news. She gave Amanda all of the details so she didn't have to call back to hear the details, but knew that she would call anyway.

"Do you think Katie and Roger are going to hook up? God, I hate that term, but you know what I mean. They seemed to really hit it off, huh?" Samantha said.

"Could be. I'm not good at paying attention to other people when you're in my presence," Craig said. Samantha beamed back at him.

"Oooh. Now that's a compliment. Come over here and put some lips behind those words." Samantha motioned her finger, directing him toward her. With her other hand she pulled the sheets back on the bed where they held their private celebration. The champagne was never touched.

Chapter XVII

*L*unar! I missed you!" Samantha bent down and held out her arms. "Pleph." Lunar's tongue caught Samantha's teeth as they bundled together on the living room floor. Amanda stayed with Lunar at Samantha's house while they were gone to make things easier with the food, bed, and toys. "You didn't run away at all did — pleph" another lick to the mouth.

Craig came down the stairs and joined them.

"Your bags are all upstairs in the bedroom. I'm going to run back to my place and take care of a few things there; get my mail and stuff. I'll call you later, okay?" He knelt down and gave Samantha a kiss, which Lunar joined in on. "Yuck, Looney! Keep the tongue away, girl," he said, yet patting her on the head.

"Bye, hun," Samantha said. She had thanked him a hundred times during the trip and on the way home from the city. He had been her number one supporter and teacher along the way, and she loved that about him. When she heard the door close and his engine start she turned back to Lunar and said, "Let's go unpack lil' girl."

When everything was either in the laundry, in a drawer, or back in the bathroom,

Samantha lay down on her bed and closed her eyes. Lunar tucked up next to her, providing warmth. She replayed the trip in her mind, still in disbelief that everything she wrote about came to be. While she managed to build upon the positive attitude she aspired to, it was still miraculous that her life was where it was, and that, she discovered, was the way the universe worked. While some may find her pie-in-the-sky approach silly or too optimistic, she was a living example that in, staying positive and holding faith, one can indeed make a living and no one could argue that fact with her.

Samantha reached over, picked up her cell phone and dialed.

"Hi Mom," she said into the phone when she heard her mother answer on the other end. "Yes, New York was great. I wanted to wait to tell everyone, but the book did really well at auction. Besides my agent, I've landed a terrific editor at the publishing house." Samantha listened for a moment. "Yes Mom, the money is great. It really is, and I'm very happy." Then, "Yes, Craig went with me. We stayed at the Four Seasons." Pause, "Yes, the money is great Mom. Don't worry. I'm in a two book deal with them so I have a lot of work to do now that I'm back home." She sat up on her bed, ready to end the call. "Lunar's fine. Amanda stayed with her while we were gone. Say hi to Dad and I'll call soon."

There, that was over. She knew that they would relay everything she said to Jane, but she called her anyways and when her call went right to voicemail, Samantha left a message with all of the details. Since she had disengaged from them, more or less, she knew they wouldn't ask for specifics. They didn't have the right to.

Samantha put the phone down and went to run a hot bath. Having been spoiled at the Four Seasons, she rediscovered the luxury of baths. While the tub filled, she picked out a magazine to read and bath oils to add. When she flipped through the pile of magazines that she hadn't touched in months, a card fell out onto the floor and landed by her feet. When she picked up the cream envelope, she noted that it hadn't been open. Flipping it to the front, her heart skipped a beat when she saw Robert's name on the return address. The stamped date showed that it was mailed the week that he came by the coffee shop. It must have gotten stuck in the magazine while in the mailbox. Her name and address were written in almost calligraphy style handwriting, but his return address was a pre-addressed sticker sponsoring the SPCA. The dog on the sticker was a German Shepherd resembling Prince. Samantha smiled at the irony. Her pinky slid though the small gap at the top of the envelope and tore it open. Inside the card pictured a black and white image of a flower, and inside it read:

"Dear Samantha,

I know you don't understand why I had to break up with you. The relationship wasn't going anywhere and neither of us seemed to care enough to say or do something to bring it to the next level. There were times when I tried and it didn't work for one reason or another and times that I felt that you wanted to try and it was again thrown off track. I decided that maybe we needed to step aside and see if missing one another would spark the relationship into action. Does that make sense?

Then I saw you at the movie theater with someone else and realized how much I missed you. Sometimes it takes that to happen, I guess. After the incident at the coffee shop, I knew you had moved on, but I still needed the closure, and hence this letter.

Best of luck to you and
your writing career. I know
you have it in you to do
great things.
Robert"

Samantha sat back down on the bed and read the letter again. She had been wrong all along about the reasons for him leaving her. Why hadn't he, why hadn't she, said or done something back then to correct it? Her gut and heart told her the answer...that it wasn't meant to be. She loved Craig and wouldn't trade him for the world. He was what she asked the Universe for in all of her positive journal requests. Her life as it was had been created by her and she was incredibly happy. This, however, was the final thread and it was cut now. She was one-hundred-percent free.

The water welcomed her as she dipped first her toe, then her legs and the rest into the tub. It wasn't as luxurious as the soaking tub at the hotel, but for here and now, she made it so. Opening *Writer's Digest* magazine, she indulged herself in reading about other authors and some writing tips. Her toes played with the faucet at the other end of the tub and Lunar slept on the bathmat. Steam coated the windows and mirrors. Silence, she realized, filled the room. New York had been a bustle of commotion, activity, sirens, and excitement; while all of it had been incredible, the quiet grounded her.

A creek on the steps broke the silence. Lunar's ears perked up and with the next creek, so did her head. Samantha grabbed the towel from the rack just as the bathroom door peeled open.

"Who's there?" Samantha demanded. The single red rose that peaked through the open crack immediately ceased her stance. Lunar's tail thumped back and forth against either side of her body as she nudged her nose through the crack of the door from inside the bathroom. "You scared me!" Samantha announced when the door opened wider and Craig exposed the rest of the roses.

"Well then, dear, you shouldn't leave the front door unlocked while you're in the tub. Or the bed, for that matter." He grinned from behind the roses.

"It's a good thing you come bearing those. They're gorgeous!" Samantha stood up from the tub and wrapped the towel around her. "Thank you."

"I'll take them downstairs and put them in a vase for you," he said after kissing her on the cheek.

"I didn't think you were coming back so soon."

"Ah, you mean the whole naked in the tub thing wasn't for me?" He tugged her towel off, causing her to screech as the cold draft from the bedroom met the warmth of her naked, still wet, body. He reached over and wrapped her in his arms, kissed her on the head, and rewrapped the towel around her before going back downstairs. In the bedroom, Samantha pulled a robe from her closet and replaced the towel with it. Her hair was already pulled up in a ponytail. On the bed lay the card from Robert. She picked it up one last time and tossed it in the garbage can before going downstairs.

Chapter XVIII

"*T*rain leaves in an hour. Almost ready?" Craig cradled his home phone between his shoulder and cheek.

"Yup! You're picking me up, right?" Samantha asked.

"Be there in twenty."

Craig's agent landed him a book deal with Warner Books, and as such, they were going back into the city — only a week after Samantha's celebration — to work the deal out and sign the contract.

Samantha needed a break from working on *Fresh Fruit, Fresh Men*. The first few rounds of drafts were done and she was at a point where she needed to step away from its words for a while. They were so imbedded in her conscious that they were starting to stifle her. New York City would be the perfect escape. She knew that Craig had taken care of all of the details, leaving her worry free.

Samantha's advance, minus her agent's fees, sat securely in her bank account. She was working on a long term investment plan with a financial planner in town that Craig recommended. There were things she wanted to take care of — possibly paying off the mortgage on the cottage and purchasing a new car. The rest she'd invest and those were the details they were working on. It was surreal having that much money. She knew that when the next bank statement arrives it would help settle it in her mind...seeing the comma between the six digits. That was what she looked forward to!

The duffle bag Samantha packed for the trip would be replaced with a nicer one while shopping in the city. This one's zipper was about to break and the nylon had grown flimsy...definitely not worthy of her stays at the Four Seasons. She pulled two of her favorite sweaters off the shelf in her closet and tucked them into the bag atop the rest of her clothing. A dress hung on the back of her bathroom door in a bag—that was going to be harder to transport on the train, but she didn't want it scrunched up in the duffle bag.

Lunar sat at the end of the bed—head resting on her crossed paws, eyes on every move Samantha made. Whenever Samantha brushed by her, Lunar's tail wagged—hovering just above the bed.

"We won't be gone long, Looney. I promise. You have fun with Amanda. I'll be back in no time," Samantha assured Lunar on the last passing before grabbing the duffle bag and dress. Lunar leaped off the bed and followed Samantha down the steps and to the front door. When Samantha opened the door and let Lunar out, she spotted Craig climbing out of his car.

"Just about ready?" he asked, bending over to greet Lunar. His smiled up at Samantha who stood leaning against the doorway.

"Almost. Let me grab my stuff. Keep an eye on her, will you?"

A minute later Samantha came out with her bag and dress, a coat draped across her arm. She let Lunar back in and gave her a bone to gnaw on until Amanda arrived that evening.

"I'll take those," Craig loaded her bag in the back next to his, draped the dress across them, and opened her door for her. She kissed him before settling into the passenger seat. He closed her door, ran around to the driver's side, and they were off.

The train ride to the city took just over an hour. Grand Central Station was crowded with business suits dodging to and fro. Craig took hold of Samantha's hand and led her through the Lexington Avenue exit where he hailed a cab.

"Four Seasons, please," Craig told the driver once they were situated in the back seat. The recent snowfall left the city streets slushed with pockets of black and white iced snow. The store windows passed by at 30 miles-per-hour as the cabby dodged between and around traffic. A blur of red and pink Valentine's decorations flashed through the glass windows, contrasting with the gray buildings.

The warm welcome from the staff and the heat of the hotel lobby was welcoming. A

248

bellhop loaded their bags on a cart; Samantha waited with him while Craig checked in and a few minutes later they entered the same room they stayed in the last time.

"Almost feels like coming home," Samantha said. "Look at the snow in the park! It's beautiful!" she exclaimed from the windowsill. She drew the curtains open as far open as possible.

"Shall we grab a bite to eat before my meeting?" Craig was meeting Roger at four o'clock that afternoon. Samantha was already planning a trip to Bloomingdales while he was in his meeting. Later, after dinner, the three of them were meeting Katie for drinks.

"Lunch sounds perfect. There's a little place down the street we can try. Looked like they had sandwiches." Samantha hung her dress in the closet, ran a brush through her hair and touched up her lip gloss. "Do you think Katie and Roger started dating? Has he said anything?"

"No he hasn't. But, it hasn't been that long since we were here," Craig stuck his head in the bathroom door where she stood over the sink. "I'm sure we'll find out this evening."

*****

Bloomingdales was packed...*probably all of the Valentine's Day shoppers*, Samantha thought. One of the reasons she wanted to shop while Craig met with Roger was because she'd been so busy—Valentine's Day crept up on her and

249

she didn't have time to pick out something at home. She knew the options in the city would be better, too.

The men's department sported manikins draped in fine suits with bright red ties— one speckled with hearts others striped like a candy cane. A display of cashmere sweaters caught her eye.

"May I help you?"

Samantha turned to find a strikingly handsome Italian salesman behind her. His dark curls sat tight atop his head and his even darker eyes waited for her answer.

"I guess so. I'm looking for a Valentine's Day present for my boyfriend. I'd like it to be special, but I'm not sure what to get him. Maybe a dark red cashmere sweater?"

"That would be a fine choice, Madame." He held up one of the sweaters then checked the tag. "What size might he be?"

"He's a medium. I prefer the v-neck over the crew."

The salesman put down the first sweater and fished out a v-neck.

"Here were go," he handed her a medium, cranberry colored sweater.

Samantha held it up to her face—so soft. Deciding on it, she handed it back to the salesman and asked him to wrap it.

Back on Broadway, she hailed a cab.

"Four Seasons," she said when she climbed into the back seat of the first cab to pull over. Her phone rang from deep insider her purse.

"Hello?"

"Hey! It's me! How's the trip going?" Amanda's voice was higher pitched than normal.

"It's great. I just picked up a cashmere sweater for Craig and am heading back to the hotel to meet him." Samantha checked her watch. Four o'clock. He'd be back in their room within an hour, then they were going out to dinner, just the two of them. She told Amanda about the train ride in and asked about Lunar. When the cab pulled up in front of the hotel, they hung up, agreeing that Samantha would call her the next day with an update.

*****

The hostess seated Samantha and Craig at a private table in the corner. It was a bit early for dinner in New York City, which made their corner spot that much quieter. Craig pulled her chair out for her and took his seat across the table. The waiter handed them their menus, reported that he'd be back, and walked away. Samantha planned on giving Craig his sweater and a card when they returned to their room later that evening.

The menu was filled with delicious sea food options and plenty of vegetarian dishes. Samantha scanned the pages in search of something light. She didn't want to fill up and go into a food coma for the rest of the evening. Deciding on a salmon dish, she put the menu down and looked up at Craig. He had been watching her, but she wasn't sure for how long.

"What?" she asked.

"Nothing."

"Nothing? You were watching me."

"Aren't I allowed to stare at the woman I love?" He winked an Aussie-style wink at her and shook out his napkin before placing it in his lap.

"How can I argue with that?" Samantha took her turn and watched him as he read the menu.

The night before, while lying in bed, he said, "You have beautiful eyes, Samantha. They're deep and soulful." Now, watching as he read the menu, she noticed how the light struck his eyes. She had always preferred brown eyes, and still she concluded that the Universe derived the shade of his brown eyes from a custom-designed color palette. They were soft, intelligent, and loving—not the cold connotation traditionally represented as brown being boring.

The salmon ended up being the perfect choice. It was tender and light, the perfect accent to the evening.

"I've ordered a special dessert to be delivered to the hotel room, so you'll have to wait," Craig announced.

"Hmmm. Does it involve chocolate?" Samantha returned his earlier Aussie-style wink.

"It might. No other hints though." Craig smiled a closed-mouth smile and nodded at her. This mannerism of his assured a delightful dessert. That was one of his facial notions that made her fall for him. The closed-mouth-smile with the reassuring-nod. He had mastered it and she devoured it like an ice-cream cone on the fourth of July. It let her know all was right in her world, and she was certain he didn't know the impact it had on her over the months. She didn't want to bring it up, afraid that he'd try to hard to do it, or worse, might be embarrassed enough that he'd stop. The funny thing was that she found herself doing it with other people. One day while she was driving and talking to Amanda, she caught herself in the motion of it. In that moment she knew he'd become a part of her in a way that no one else ever had, and she wondered if he had notably picked up any of her mannerisms.

"Shall we go?" Craig finished signing the credit card receipt.

"Ready. Thank you. That was delicious."

During the cab ride back to the hotel, she held his hand and looked out the window. His hand felt balmy in her palm, a comfortable feeling that she was sure dropped her blood pressure with just his touch. In fact, she believed, there were studies that addressed the effects of a gentle touch between a man and a woman. She tucked the thought away in her mind to research, as it would be great material for a book.

*****

Craig held tight to her hand in the elevator and to their room. When they entered Samantha's mouth dropped. A bouquet of white roses sat on a table in the middle of the room. Red rose pedals scattered across the bed, and a bottle of champagne sat on a cart accompanied by two bowls of chocolate mousse. A small box sat between the two desserts.

Samantha raised her hand to her mouth.

"Are we in the right room?" she asked, half laughing, half serious.

Craig reached over to the table and picked up the box. Handing it to her, he said, "Samantha, I never thought I'd meet someone that I could look into her eyes and know I'd want to spend the rest of my life with. I didn't think such a woman existed or that I would deserve her. Then there you were. Sitting in the coffee shop day after day working so hard on your writing without another care in the world. I knew then that you'd get me. That you'd understand me. And although I knew that, you've far exceeded what I envisioned when I first lay eyes on you. You compliment who I am and I can't imagine a day without you, let alone my life. Will you marry me?"

The tears of joy that streamed down Samantha's cheeks contrasted drastically to the ones she shed only months ago. The tear-stained pillowcases had long been replaced, and now the tears rolling off her cheeks and onto the floor below represented a rebirth into a time of happiness and deserving. The Universe had delivered. She long since realized her deservingness and had learned that when her desires were manifested, 99% of the work was done in other dimensions of the Universe — places beyond our physical awareness — before they came to fruition in our world. Relinquishing control and holding faith, she learned, was really the best option for creating what she wanted in her life. Her journaling, followed by going about her day, had proven that.

Samantha looked deep into Craig's eyes and gave him her best closed-mouthed-smiling-nod.

Chapter XIX

Ten Months Later:

*S*amantha loved being pregnant more than she thought she would. Having Craig as a husband made every part easier — he catered to her every whim, made sure she was comfortable while sleeping. Some nights she awoke to find him next to her, leaning on one arm, and holding his other hand on her belly. When he looked down at her they shared a smile, an unspoken love that radiated through their child. She often thought of what the baby would look like, hoping it would have his eyes, his bone structure. The idea of either a boy or girl was appealing.

"What are you thinking about?" Craig interrupted her silence one morning. She was sitting on the couch, hand rested on her belly.

"Just that I'm the luckiest soon-to-be mom in the world because you." She smiled up at him as he approached the couch and sat down beside her.

"This child is the lucky one." He squeezed her foot. "Tea?"

"Sounds perfect."

Craig had given up his apartment in town and moved into Samantha's cabin just before the wedding. They were in the process of looking at houses closer to the city since Craig was often traveling to meet with his agent and editor...he didn't want to be too far away from Samantha and the baby. Samantha's first book was in printing and pre-sales mode. Her second book was almost through final edits — the goal was to deliver the manuscript before the baby was delivered. After that she was taking a sabbatical to enjoy motherhood.

"Can you bring me my journal?" Samantha called to the kitchen. Getting up off the couch was growing more difficult as she grew. She'd also started writing in her positive journal during the day when she had some downtime because by time she went to bed she was exhausted. While she'd created everything that she desired in her life, she now journaled new ideas about the desires of her growing family.

"Here you go...one cup of tea and one journal." Craig placed the tea on the table and handed her the journal with her "Valentine's Pen." A kiss on the forehead topped it off before he announced he was going to take Lunar for a walk. The fall leaves were mid-color change, Lunar was full grown, and Craig had created a defined trail in the woods for them to hike on. Until they moved to their new house, the cabin proved to be a warm place to start their marriage and the pregnancy happened so quickly, it was a good thing they weren't in the midst of moving yet.

"Enjoy your walk!" Samantha called as she heard the closing of the door.

Settling deeper into the couch she thought about how nice it was to know that the front door would soon open again and he'd be back through it. Not like the other men. She held her pen to the journal's paper:

I am grateful.

Heather Hummel

Heather Hummel is an author who specializes in the genre of Body, Mind, & Soul with an emphasis on life transitions. Her previous book, *Gracefully: Looking and Being Your Best at Any Age* (McGraw Hill, 2008), was coauthored with her mother, Valerie Ramsey. Heather's spiritual essays have been published in *Blue Ridge Anthology* and *Messages of Hope and Healing.*

Heather is a graduate of the University of Virginia (Bachelor of Interdisciplinary Studies), is working toward her PhD in Metaphysical Sciences, and is a writing

coach and editor for aspiring writers. Visit Heather's website at
www.heatherhummel.net

PRAISE FOR

Through Hazel Eyes

Heather Hummel
(PathBinder Publishing)
*2009 New York Book
Festival
1st Honorable Mention
in the Romance Genre*

"Plan on saying, 'Just one more chapter.'"
- Fritz Fanke, University of Virginia

"This is a story of transformation and
growth."
- Caroline Collins, Café Mojo

"It is captivating and intriguing. Once I
started reading this book it was very difficult
to put down. The characters are very real
and you can walk in their shoes!
Great Book!"
- Vickie Borchers, Wachovia Bank

-

"This is a "could not put it down"
rainy day book or beach book."
- Fred Scott, The Bolles School

PRAISE FOR

GRACEFULLY: LOOKING AND BEING YOUR BEST AT ANY AGE
Valerie Ramsey with Heather Hummel
(McGraw-Hill)

"[Gracefully] offers guidance on how to maximize good health at every stage of life"!
- **Body & Soul Magazine**, April, 2008

"*Gracefully* is simply wonderful. Valerie Ramsey is living proof that being older than 50 can be exciting, healthy, and sexy."

-Christiane Northrup, MD Author of *Mother-Daughter Wisdom, The Wisdom of Menopause,* and *Women's Bodies, Women's Wisdom*

"I like the snappy way this gal thinks. She sends out a powerful message!"
-Rue McClanahan, Actress

BE THE WRITER
ADVICE ON BECOMING A WRITER

Heather Hummel

*O*ther than "What do you write?" I am often asked "*How did you succeed?*" Besides being an author, I fill the role as an editor and a writing coach to aspiring writers who look to me for answers to the latter question. Some of them come to me feeling defeated while others are newbies with high expectations. Yet, my response to both is the same, **"Be the Writer!"**

Easy to say, "Be the Writer" and really not that hard to do if your heart is in it.

To help *you* put *your* heart in it, here are some tidbits I learned along the way:

1. Be creative when finding places for your work.

- **Newsletters**: I started out as the Editor-in-Chief of a University of Virginia alumni newsletter. I did everything from writing the articles to the design/layout and distribution. Having "The University of Virginia" on

- **Regional magazines**: These magazines hire freelance writers all the time. Check the websites of your local regional magazines for submission guidelines. This is a great place to build your "clips" because no matter what you *want* to write, building your portfolio counts. If the editor likes your work, they will keep you busy!

- **Contests**: Enter contests! Follow the guidelines, polish your work, and be willing pay the entry fees. You never know, and if you win or receive any recognition it can carry a lot of weight. There are several contests per year and many are listed in the Writer's Marketplace.

- **Join Writing Groups and Attend Conferences**: Writing guilds and organizations (such as the International Women's Writing Guild, or regional venues such as Richmond, Virginia's *James River Writers*), put you in contact with other writers. There are several annual conferences nationwide that give you the opportunity to meet other writers and to pitch your work to agents.

2. Build your platform.

These words make every new writer cringe. And then there are those who aren't familiar with the meaning or significance of the word "platform." No matter how unfair it sounds, having a platform (your credentials and beyond) matters.

Fiction and nonfiction are two different beasts. For fiction, winning those contests (especially the notable ones) helps tremendously. For nonfiction, who and how many people you know, your venue, how well you know your topic (expertise), and being in the public eye matters. One angle I used to build my platform was approaching literary festivals about being a guest author on their panels. What was so great about being on a panel was sharing the stage with other authors. The spotlight wasn't completely off me and our energy fed one another. The more speaking engagements about your topic you do, the more comfortable you become doing them and at the same time you can add the credits to your queries and proposals. Keep your website and blog up to date with your calendar.

3. Write a great novel or an awesome book proposal - then know where and how to shop it.

Do your research. Again, Writer's Marketplace is a tool that should be on every new author's desk.

- Know that the majority of publishers (especially the big houses) only accept submissions from agents (i.e. you need an agent).

- Know that a novel must be complete and as great as you can make it before you query agents.

- Know that nonfiction requires a well constructed book proposal and sample material, but the manuscript does not need to be complete.

- Know that every agent has different submission guidelines and represents different genres. Respect their guidelines and the genres they represent, or you will likely be rejected. (Most have their guidelines posted on their website.)

It's no secret that agents have about a 91 to 96% rejection rate, and I would venture to guess that the majority of these rejections are simply from writers not doing their homework. Don't spend hours, months, years working on a book and only minutes preparing it for an agent. Your work deserves better than that and your agent deserves your respect. Know the guidelines, make your manuscript sparkle (hiring a professional editor is worth every penny), and be professional...always.

4. Attitude is everything.

Despite everything I listed above, the number one success tool you have for becoming a writer is your attitude. A positive attitude (without arrogance) will take you places you never imagined you could go. This goes for all aspects of life, not just being a writer.

5. Think Body, Mind and Soul.

Body - write! Find time to write. I don't believe in writer's block, and as such I've never experienced it. There is always something to write about. Not only is my license plate (on my antique Volvo P1800E that was my grandmother's) **2KWPD,** but that's my goal as a writer - to write or edit 2,000 words per day.

Be the Writer

Mind - be creative in all aspects of being a writer. Use your brain not only with your work, but where and how to find a home for it.

Soul - the essence of being a writer means you feel it to the core of your being. I know, what you're thinking - sounds hokey - but I have to tell you, it's true!

Apparently George Martin (Beatles producer) was once asked, "What advice do you have for those pursuing a career in the music industry?"
George responded, "I would discourage them."
"Why? Look at what a great lifestyle you have?" continued the inquisition.
"Because those who *can* be discouraged *ought* to be discouraged," George said.

Think about it.

Writing has always been my passion. My grandmother was an author and freelance writer, and as a teen I used to send her short stories that she critiqued and mailed back to me. Originally I wanted to be a photojournalist, but I was always a better writer than photographer. At the very least, I've kept a journal since eighth grade and took writing classes along the way, including the Institute of Children's Literature (in my early twenties).

I resigned from teaching (high school English) to become a writer in early 2005, my 40th birthday present to myself. At the time I didn't know much about being a writer except *how* to write. I spent the next two years eating, breathing, and reading about the business end of being a writer. I read books like *Publishers Marketplace*, *Write the Perfect Book Proposal: 10 That Sold and Why*, and every issue of *Writers Digest* magazine (of which I had been a subscriber of for decades). To hone my writing skills, I joined writing groups and took workshops through the Charlottesville Writing Center (for more information on participating in writing workshops, see Writing Workshop Etiquette on my website). I even enter the National Novel Writing Month contest every year (NANOWRIMO)!

I landed an agent by writing a knock-out book proposal and being positive, pleasant and professional. We sold the book to McGraw Hill within a short amount of time based on my mother's platform. She had already proven herself as a 67 year old model, but I still had to prove myself as a writer who could make it at this level. And I did. I wrote the book in the time promised without sacrificing quality. I communicated with the editor professionally and responded to all of his requests. In the end, he was thrilled with the final manuscript and I was validated in what I already knew - that I was a writer.

Everything I did during those years was about becoming a writer. That's what I mean when I say, **"Be the writer."** You have to care, you have to crave it, you have to want it more than anything, and most of all, you have to believe in yourself.

Several of my clients have succeeded in finding an agent or publisher, while others are well on their way. Ask any of them (or read their testimonials on PathBinder Publishing's website) and they will surely tell you that besides the edits, besides the proposal tweaks, I teach them the importance of positive thinking. Fortunately, they've been quick learners or came to me with the right attitude already, which has been what makes being a writing coach extremely rewarding!

When I tell them, **"Be the Writer"** they understand it and for each, the persona of "writer" is quite different. That's what makes this such an amazing field to be in. Everyone has a story about how they made it - the stories are as different as the number of books out there. Make your own story.

For More Information on Heather's Coaching for Writer's Program, contact Heather Hummel at Heather@HeatherHummel.net

Be the Writer